Acclaim for

Night Hues

by Gwendolyn Jensen-Woodard

Night Hues settings and drama, mysteries and surprises, coupled with the author's eloquent storytelling, gave me hours of true pleasure. I will be following this author and eagerly awaiting more of her stories.

Chris Davidson

I've read two of Gwendolyn's short stories, Nightlife and Heart of Night, so when I saw the cover reveal for *Night Hues,* I knew I was in for a good time! I was not disappointed. Twists and turns abound. Lilah is incredibly strong and intense, and along with her 'unusual' nature, is someone to get to know better- maybe as a character/friend.

Donna Marker

Night Hues

by

Gwendolyn Jensen-Woodard

Vanilla Heart Publishing

Night Hues

by Gwendolyn Jensen-Woodard

Copyright 2017 Gwendolyn Jensen-Woodard

Published by: Vanilla Heart Publishing

www.VanillaHeartPublishing.com

10121 Evergreen Way, 25-156

Everett, WA 98204 USA

This book is a work of fiction. Names, characters, places, and incidents are either the product of the author's imagination or are used fictitiously, and any resemblance to places, events, or persons living or dead is purely coincidental.

ISBN-13: 978-1-937227-11-1   ISBN-10: 1-937227-11-1

10 9 8 7 6 5 4 3 2 1 First Edition

First Printing, March 2017

Printed in the United States of America

Table of Contents

Table of Contents (*cont'd*)

Dedication

With love to Rhiannon and Bridget, my amazing daughters.

Acknowledgments

My family, who gave me the peace and understanding to write a book, and to K'Lee, without her gentle prods and understanding, this would never have been published.

Night Hues

by

Gwendolyn Jensen-Woodard

Prologue

The call was late, or early depending on the point of view. The east was changing from the deepest blue of midnight, to the dark aqua of the ocean at night. The city was beginning slowly to come alive, for those who lived in the sun. Lights blinked on in buildings, and cars raced by. The sound of the wind and rain on I5, being mere feet from the alley where the victim lay, moaned lamentations for a man who will never see another sunrise.

Lieutenant Lilah Evans stood carefully, taking a half-step back from the corpse. As an experienced homicide detective, she headed up any nighttime murders, though it was her prerogative to hand off some to the Detectives in homicide. Lilah kept the strange ones herself. She viewed it as a challenge. The corpse this night looked like any normal murder. Or it would, if Lilah were human.

Detective Allen Davies, newly assigned to her squad. He was new to Seattle, but he wasn't green, and back in St. Louis he'd had the authority. Here, Lilah had rank, and for some reason that put a chip on his shoulder. Almost like a grudge, he didn't want to see the Lieutenant do a better job than himself. It might have been colored with a smidge of misogyny. Allen Davies didn't know anything about Lilah first hand, and decided on the spot, that she'd earned her badge. In Lilah's opinion, it was a great way to be a pain in her ass.

"Dazzle me, Lieutenant Lilah." She hated it when people did that, used her first name instead of her last. She'd earned her title the hard way, like most of the department. It was a matter of respect. Detective Davies, like anyone else who did it, was trying to make it an insult.

Detective Davies stood back, arms crossed, and waited. Lilah nearly scowled at him, but knew it wouldn't help. Too many times she'd stood next to a crime scene, and stood for the dead, having to prove her knowledge to someone else.

"It's obviously a homicide, Davies. Blunt trauma to the back of the head, would have hurt like hell had he been alive to feel it." Lilah snapped absently picking at her gloves, bent and probed his head, noticing there wasn't enough blood around the wound. Davies started to smile condescendingly and began to open his mouth. Ignoring him, Lilah went on her with examination of the body and scene.

"However, the blunt trauma was not the cause of death. This man was bludgeoned after he died. The ligature marks around his neck, indicate that he was strangled. They're light, but deep, meaning it was something thin, more likely wire than rope or article of clothing. Someone was hoping the Seattle Police Department was stupid, and would assume this was a common mugging." Lilah indicated the wallet thrown by the man's feet, open, and empty of money, cards or ID.

"Instead, I believe this was premeditated. Otherwise, he would have just been hit, robbed and left for dead." Lilah knew there was a bit of a blood trail, slowly washing away in the rain, and invisible to the eye in the dark, wet alley. She smelled it, almost tasting it: salty and metallic. Knowing she

16

couldn't prove a smell to Detective Davies, Lilah was glad for more, visual physical evidence.

"Under his head, and shoulders, down his back and to his feet, there were several small drops of blood, smeared down through his clothing. There's not enough around his head, even for that wound. He wasn't killed here. He was brought here.

"Most likely he was dragged by his arms, to be left in the alley like refuse," Lilah finished, and stood, daring Detective Davies, with his gloves still on, to turn the body over, finding the small evidence Lilah described. Something he'd overlooked. Letting the body rock back to his back, Allen stood up, eyes slightly narrowed. He threw his gloves in a bag offered by one of the forensic team members, and started to walk away. Lilah tossed her gloves as well, before motioning for the rest of the teams to finish with the body, and followed the Detective.

"I heard you were smart, Evans." He made his way back to his late model, black sedan.

"I heard stories that you were good, sometimes too good, but I didn't believe them. Word is that you often take cases that others don't want, because they're strange, dangerous or both. No one, and I mean no one, is that good." He leaned on the car, and stared at Lilah for a moment. "People who insist they work only nights, especially once they hit Lieutenant, are often a bit strange. Paranoid, nuts, stupid, burnt out, or something else" he paused, "Which are you?"

Lilah laughed but it wasn't tinged even a little with humor, which had him blinking back in the darkness. Whatever he had expected, it was not that.

"I am Lieutenant Lilah Evans, the head of homicide on night shift. I was offered a daytime position, however I like the night. It is never boring, because when the sun goes down, the real life of this city begins. I like the excitement, I like the people, hell, I like the smell. As for strange cases, didn't you know, the freaks come out at night?" She could have said more, about how the dead haunt her. How death was her bane, and had been for more years than Davies had been alive. But none of it would have mattered.

Detective Davies stayed quiet, and she saw his face harden. Not only didn't he get the reference, he had made up his mind about her. Lilah guessed he wasn't a classic rock fan.

"I don't care what you like, or don't like! Or when the 'freaks', as you say, come out. I'm here to do my job. And I don't work for you!"

"Actually, if you got a good look at my badge, that's exactly what it means, Detective. The nights are mine. I do a good job, I close many of my cases, and I really don't need this shit from you." This time she looked him in the eye, hard to do as he had at least a foot on her, at 6'5". Even in the dark, his blue eyes glinted. Yet Lilah wasn't done.

"This isn't just my job, this is who I am."

Detective Allen Davies headed for his car but Lilah had more to say. She'd had it with his type.

"This is my case Allen. I'll do the paperwork, and I'll do the follow up. You may have been first on scene, but you are new to homicide." Lilah turned to watch the ME take away the body, and then turned back.

"When I get the Medical Examiner's report, I'll share it with you, because that's my damned job. If you push me on this, I'll bench you. Then watch it from the squad room. I hope we are clear, because right now, I'm done with you."

18

Lilah turned, stalking to her old, white VW Bug with tinted windows, letting him scurry into his sedan, and drive off into the burgeoning day. Lilah didn't give a damn what he thought of her, as long as Detective Davies stayed out of her way. He didn't know her, and was new to Lilah's prescient, and as such, Lilah couldn't waste her time on Allen's "hurt" feelings. Instead she cared about the dead man who was trundling toward the morgue in the ME van. He had all her attention now.

Once the scene was cleared, the sun was slowly peeking through, turning night to day; the blue was fading to purple and then pink as Lilah raced to the parking garage at the station. She knew better than to be caught in the sun.

It didn't take long for Lilah to file the report. Luckily, the windows in the Police Department were covered several years ago with very strong wooden blinds. It had a two-fold purpose as far as Lilah was concerned: it kept out the rabid reporters and the UV rays.

Lilah left her car at the police station; her reason was always "so I can get it quickly from work". It was much safer than taking the streets home. . Even in Seattle, the sun could be a little damaging. It would just be a nasty burn, compared to say a homo-sanguines, or a "vampire" who'd be turned to ash.

The elevator in the SPD parking garage goes to a basement level, leading to a sewer opening and the sewer in turn leads to a little known path in Underground Seattle. Sure, it was a tad cliché, but it was safe. Lilah checked it out before heading back to the Pacific Northwest. Luckily, her basement apartment had an even older room underneath that was part of the Underground. She was able to go from headquarters to home without ever seeing the sun. When called in during the day, Lilah could make it in without having to explain the sunburn in the rain.

Home was her safe-haven. The small windows that once let in so little light even mold never took hold, now let in no light. The landlord didn't care that Lilah blocked them out, as long as she paid her rent on time. It had three bedrooms, one bath, and blessed, cool darkness all for a small portion of her paycheck each month. After the night with Detective Davies, she was tired and hungry. Rare, red meat was a staple. She needed a bit more protein than most people, just to keep going, and she needed the blood to survive. Lilah pulled a New York strip out of her refrigerator and gave it quick sear on each side. Since Lilah's canines' were only slightly sharper than average, she had no fangs to get in the way, making the meat easier to chew.

Sitting at her small oaken table, dinner was a chance to reflect. Lilah was sure she'd missed something on the body today, as she'd allowed Detective Davies to rattle her too much. She'd call Dr. Drusilla Collins, the head coroner, in the morning. If she'd missed it, Dru would catch it. Shaking her head, Lilah felt sad. If Lilah's life had been less complicated, she might be able to call Dr. Drusilla Collins her friend. Instead, the good doctor was just a colleague. Lilah had very few close friends. It's hard to live with one foot in the world of the living and one always in the world of the dead.

Lilah's mother was human, but her father was a "homo sanguines" or "vampire" in the vernacular. That made Lilah half human, or "homo sapiens sanguines". Lilah, and anyone that might be like her, were a myth to vampire kind, and not even a blip to humans. Her mother, Lily, shouldn't have been able to give birth to a cross species baby. As far as Lilah knew, there were no other children like her.

Just as Lilah was preparing to sleep for the day, her cell phone buzzed. She tried to ignore it, because the number was unknown. But Detective Davies wasn't added yet, hadn't been added to her phone yet, and perhaps he had a new lead. Sighing, she answered it.

"Evans."

"Lilah?" Her friend Christine Blanchard's voice floated over the line, sounding strained. As she was calling from an unlisted number, something had to be wrong.

"Cris, are you okay?"

"No, I'm really not. I'm calling from the club. I need to talk to you, can I come over now?" Cris was Lilah's only friend, a human who knew her secret and still wanted to come over in the day time. That meant she didn't just want to chat over coffee. Something was wrong.

"Of course, I'll leave the door unlocked." Lilah never said "come in" when someone visited. Too many things that go bump in the night could take advantage of a little consent. Unlike her parasitic relatives, Lilah didn't need to sleep in a coffin, or seem to die at dawns first light. She just really didn't do well in the sun. And since she could afford very few friends, Lilah didn't want to alienate the one she had.

Cris hung up without a good-bye, presumably on her way. Lilah got up slowly, aching a little with the lack of sleep, and started some coffee. Not that Lilah drank coffee, but Cris did. And there was nothing wrong with a little hospitality.

Lilah had met Christine on a case. At the time, Cris had been a kid, prostituting on the Ave, trying to get by. A guy had come by, busted her and her room-mate up. Lilah was the first on scene. The stupid guy jumped her, high on some drug that kept him from staying down. Normal fighting wasn't working, so without thinking, she'd picked him up, and tossed him out the door and bounced him down some stairs. It was all for his and the girls' safety of course. Then she got him cuffed and out of there.

A few days later, Cris looked up Lieutenant Lilah Evans, at the station, asking to speak with her. She wanted help to get out of the life, which Lilah offered, calling shelters, finding her food, and money. Right before Cris left, she'd said "I don't know what you are exactly, but I believe you're good. So I'll keep it to myself." That was 10 years ago.

Since, Cris managed to stay out of the working girl life, instead getting her life together. And she and Lilah remained friends.

Lilah sat across from Cris at her dinner table. She noted that Cris was looking paler than herself, which was saying a lot. Cris' cup shook, and she made no attempt to bring it to her mouth. She just sat there for a few minutes, getting up the courage to talk.

"Lilah," she started, "we both know you're not all 'normal', and that's always been cool with me. After all, you're one of the good guys." Her green eyes finally lifted from the table, and met Lilah's, desperation nearly clouding the green.

"I think I met the bad ones last night. I mean like you, or sort of like you. I was the Club, dancing and singing along like I do. No real date, just having fun with friends." Since she'd gone straight, Cris started college, and was finishing up her BS in computer science. She'd made a few girlfriends' at the school, and they went out once or twice a week. A new dance and music business, Ravens, had opened down near the water three months before, and a place they'd taken to just calling "the Club".

"I was just there, and this guy tapped me on the shoulder. Asked me to dance, you know? But his eyes, I'd never seen any like them. They were blue, but they almost seemed to swirl, mixing colors. I can't even try to describe it, 'cause when I think about them, it blurs a little. I couldn't look away. He led me out, danced for a while, I don't know how long, 'cause time didn't seem to matter. Then he held my hand, taking me to the back corner, away from Lisa James and Kally Greene." Cris named her school friends, and Lilah was very afraid she knew where this story was going. Her father had similar eyes: shimmering green and gold that often changed from one moment to the next. He could never hold Lilah with them, but maybe he'd never tried. As Cris spoke, Lilah gave a silent prayer to which ever deity would listen, that she was wrong.

"In the corner, he tried to kiss me, but I pulled away. Once I did, he started speaking in a whisper, words I didn't quite understand but I couldn't help but try and listen, though he didn't try to touch me again." Cris continued, her eyes starting to mist, "After a while, he stopped, and I turned away for a moment. Another man was with Lisa, and she had a look on her face, as though was he was life, and air, and everything she'd ever need. He was tall, Lilah. Well over 6 feet, and totally not her type. She like them her size, made her feel safe. But the look she had..." Cris shook her head, trying to clear it, "The guy I was with began saying something, and I turned back. Was going to say I had to go, and get the girls' and get the hell out of there. It just felt...wrong. He nodded, and walked away, but when I turned, I couldn't find Lisa anywhere. I found Kally by herself, peeved that we'd ditched her, but Lisa never came back. I waited for her, but the sun came up, the Club closed, and she never came out." The last was a half-wail, giving Cris the sound of a small girl, rather than the 25 year old she was.

"Cris, are you sure she didn't just head out for a passionate night?" Lilah had only met Cris' friends once, and had no idea what Lisa would or wouldn't do. She hoped that it was a normal pick-up and regret situation

"No." Cris was firm, even though the tears were streaming down her face. "Lisa was waiting for marriage. Cute, actually, and I envied her a little, since I can't do that. She wouldn't have just gone off, Lilah. We were supposed to take a test this morning. We were all going to crash at my place, and then head to class." With everything Christine had been through, Lilah knew this was sincere. Cris knew evil too, even if it was merely human. Something about those men had set off her creep alert.

"Have you called her place?"

Cris nodded.

"Listen, what else do you remember?" Lilah knew there was no going straight to the police. A college girl is gone for a few hours after going to a club isn't exactly a missing person, at least, not legally. "I need to know, anything stick out besides the eyes?"

Christine closed her eyes for a moment. After having been on the streets, she learned to watch her surroundings, and the people in them. Only this time, Lilah was afraid Cris didn't get the chance. Then again, anything might help.

"The guy that talked to me, I can't see him. I try, and I get lightheaded. Black hair, like yours, I think. And the blue eyes, my height, maybe a little taller?" Cris is 5'6", so this guy wasn't even average height. The other guy, however.

"He was tall, like I said. Blond hair? Verging on white, I think. He doesn't blur as much, but I didn't get a great look at him. Couldn't see his eyes at all. He looked out of place in the club, almost elegant. Like he was over dressed, in a tux maybe?" She opened her eyes, and sighed.

"That's all I can remember Lilah, and I'm not sure how it'll help. But you've got to do something. These weren't normal guys. And Lisa, she's still gone." Lilah knew Cris was right, though she wished otherwise.

"Cris, if you want to crash here, it's cool. I promise, as soon as the sun goes down, I'll head to the club, and see if I can start there. I have a case I'm working on, but I'll squeeze this in." Lilah reached for her hand, and held it for a moment. "I promise".

Cris smiled, her pale face gaining a little color back, her black eyes drooping. "I think I'll take you up on that couch. Maybe I can help tonight?"

Lilah shook her head, "Cris, I don't think it's a good idea. In fact, you and Kally need to stay away from Ravens altogether. Please. At least until I give you the green light." Cris nodded, and Lilah knew she'd stay away and find a way to talk her friend into not going back.

As she settled on the couch, her eyes drooping, Lilah asked "what about your test?"

"I'm already passing with an A. I'm allowed to skip one. I just wasn't going to." Lilah smiled, knowing how hard she'd worked for that grade. "Good for you," was the last thing said before Lilah dropped into bed, with sleep only moments behind.

The phone rang, pulling Lilah out of a dreamless sleep. Sleeping was like that for her almost all of the time. An old lover once said it was like sleeping next to the dead. Lilah was pretty sure it wasn't a compliment.

"Evans?" Lilah kept one phone next to the bed, making it easier to answer.

"Lilah, its Dr. Collins." Dr. Drusilla Collins was the lead medical examiner. They went back several years, meeting after one of Lilah's first homicides. They got along well, though sometimes the doctor looked at Lilah, as though she knew Lilah wasn't quite normal, that she was other; however, the doctor never mentioned it.

"Good morning to you," Lilah laughed, being a night person, it was her morning.

"Lilah, the homicide that came in last night, the man found in the alley? I need you to come down and take a look at it." Dr. Collins rarely called directly after a body was brought in. Autopsies take time, but something wasn't right. Lilah pulled herself out of the sanctuary of her bed.

"What is it?"

"I can't tell you over the phone, it sounds too weird. Please just come down. After you look at it, we can call in your partner." Although that was against protocol, Lilah wasn't going to argue. She wasn't prepared to deal with Davies just yet.

"I'll be there in about 15 minutes."

"Good. Lilah, be prepared, this one is weird." Dr. Collins hung up without saying goodbye. Whatever it was, it had shaken the good doctor.

"Cris?" Lilah yelled, pulling on a pair of faded blue jeans, and a black tee. Black always went well with Lilah's complexion, and brought out the natural and varied shades of black in her hair.

"I'm making coffee." Either she'd heard the phone ring, or was already up. The fact that she waited for Lilah said she was still worrying about her friend.

"Thanks, I'll be right out." It felt like it was a cliché and against social norms in Seattle, but Lilah wasn't much one for coffee, keeping it around for the smell more than anything else. Lilah pulled her vertical shoulder holster and Sig Saur 1911 on over the tee-shirt, and then threw her dark brown jacked over it. In the pocket was her badge, and all together, she looked like a nearly respectable detective. It was a plus, that most people didn't care about fashion on the night shift. Or maybe it was that no one else really dressed up, unless slacks and dress shoes counted over her black and white Converse high-tops. Lilah decided that this was her uniform (except when the occasion called for her to be formal), choosing to think of them as part of her "police persona".

"Cris, I have to head out. You're welcome to hang here another night," she looked at Lilah, questions in her eyes. Lilah looked at Cris and sighed.

"I'll go to Ravens tonight. After I talk to Dr. Collins about a case I'm on, okay?" Cris smiled, lighting up her pretty, childlike face. Almost like a puppy after it's been given a treat.

"I'll hang here there." Cris laughed, "Besides, you have cable, and we decided we couldn't afford it."

"Lock the door behind me."

Lilah headed out. Since the sun hadn't set yet, she used the basement exit. It was free of windows and only had the exit to the Underground. Lilah moved quickly, faster than human speed, taking no more than 10 minutes to get the 6 miles to Seattle General, which happened to be the hospital that held the biggest morgue, taking all of the SPD's homicides. It wasn't too far from the police station, which was a convenience, most of the time.

It's amazing how many places in this city had lower levels. Luckily for Lilah, SG was one of them. It had been built in the '50's, made to withstand fire, and even the occasional earthquake (as opposed to many other buildings in the City), and as such had easy access from the sewers or the Underground by the boiler room. Of course, it was an old iron door that was kept padlocked and shut, but that never really was a problem. After the first time Lilah tore it off the padlock, she just repositioned it to look like it locked. Heck it even had rust spots in the right places. Once out of the boiler-room and onto the bottom most floor of the hospital, Lilah waited behind a door for two nurses to amble to the elevators, and vacate the hallway.

Once it was clear, Lilah let herself out and headed for Dr. Drusilla Collins office. Her door was cracked, and she was sitting at her desk, speaking into a small hand held tape recorder. Though the good doctor could have used newer technology, Lilah had only ever seen Dr. Dru dictate into the recorder. Dru was one of the taller women Lilah met, standing about six feet tall, beautiful brown eyes, and skin that showed ebony in dim light, and more of a chocolate in bright lights, with highlights of purple. She kept her hair short, straightened, and swept back from her face. Lilah always assumed it was so it didn't get in her way when she was working. A hair falling in the wrong place can contaminate evidence. Or, maybe, she just liked it that way. As it was, Dru was a very striking woman, who commanded attention with her body language, even though her voice was soft, like the wind on a warm spring day.

"I'm here," Lilah knocked quietly and waited for Dr. Dru to invite her in. Patient confidentiality was something the medical community took that very seriously.

"Come in Lieutenant." She motioned me into her office and to the chair in front of her desk.

"What's up Doc?" Not original, but it always made Dru smile. In her line of business, that wasn't a bad thing. The dead didn't tell many jokes.

"Do you believe in the supernatural?" It was an odd question, and one that made Lilah go very still. Was the good doctor going to ask about her origins? She hoped not.

"Like magic?" Lilah asked, watching those brown eyes, unable to read anything other than fear in them. Luckily, the fear wasn't directed at Lilah, which was good. That wasn't a conversation she wanted to have with Doctor Dru, possibly ever.

"Magic yes. But other things, things they tell us are only made up. Like werewolves or vampires." That was a word Lilah had been dreading to hear.

"I don't know. The best answer I have is: maybe. Many weird things seem to go unexplained. Why do you ask?" Lilah was careful to give a noncommittal answer. She sighed then, her lightly colored lips frowning just a little.

"Because what I'm about to show you isn't normal. I haven't seen it before, and you and I have seen some pretty terrible things." Lilah nodded, because it was true. It isn't possible to work Homicide, and no see the horrible things

29

one human can do to another. Things you never want to see or speak of again.

"Let's go," Dru stood, and grabbed a keycard from her desk. Lilah didn't have to ask where. It was the only card for the morgue where the suspected homicide cases were kept. Separate from people who died of normal things, like heart disease and car accidents. The morgue was connected to Dru's office, but the door was often kept locked. Lilah followed her in, ready to see whatever had scared the doctor.

The body was already out, in the chilled room. Temperature never bothered Lilah, always feeling the same regardless of sun, snow or the obvious rain. She could see the hairs stand up a little on Dr. Dru's arms, which clued her into the temperature of the room. Of course, it helped slow the decomposition process. "John Doe 335," the number was an indicator of how many unnamed male bodies has been through the morgue already this year.

Lilah looked at the body, now with the Y incisions, already sewn up down his body, and the blue tinge to his lips and fingers. He looked the same as he had last night: Dead.

"I read your report when the body came in. You were right, it wasn't the head wound that killed him; it was strangulation that caused his ultimate death. In fact, the head wound, though it bled a lot, was mostly superficial. A red herring I suspect."

"Been reading those detective novels again?" Lilah grinned, and Dru had the grace to blush slightly. But she went on.

"There were two things not evident during your inspections. One, you couldn't know until his labs came in, he was very anemic. He just didn't have quite enough blood inside his body. The other, I found another set of markings that you missed when the body was clothed." Lilah put on a pair of powder free polyurethane gloves, ready when the doctor was.

Dr. Dru, as gently as she could, pulled the thighs apart. Lilah ran her hands over the area. She could feel the indentations in the inner thigh.

"Now look," the doctor aimed a light at the leg, and Lilah looked at the wounds. There were two small puncture wounds over the femoral artery. They were symmetrical in shape, and less than an inch apart.

"Damn," Lilah whispered softly, knowing full well what it was. Luckily, it wasn't the bite that killed him, or there'd be extra problems in the morgue tonight.

"What is it, Lilah?" Dr. Dru looked at the Lieutenant, both hopeful and afraid that she'd have the answer.

"You're the doctor, you tell me," Lilah tried for innocent, but it came out whiny, almost pleading. John Doe 335 had been found only a few blocks from Ravens, and Lilah knew in her gut that it was the last place he'd been seen alive.

"Lilah, if I tell you what I think, it stays between us. It doesn't go on the record, and it sure as hell doesn't go to your partner or anyone else." Lilah nodded. If Doctor Dru was going to trust her, she couldn't turn her back on Dru.

"Let's sit first." They pulled the white sheet back over the body, and went to sit at the small computer area. Dru kept her voice low as she met Lilah's eyes.

"I know you've dealt with some cases that just couldn't be explained for one reason or another. Most of those cases seem to fall to you." Lilah started to interrupt, and deny it, or blame it on the night, but Dru held up a hand, stopping the protestations in their tracks.

"We've known each other too long for you to say no to that now. I've seen almost everyone you've brought in, and most of the time, I kept my mouth shut, but this time I just can't." She ran her fingers through her hair, trying to keep herself from shaking.

"Damn it girl, it looks like a vampire bite. Or at least, what they say one looks like." And there it was. The dark underground nightlife, with things no human wanted to face suddenly leapt up, and scared the hell out of a hard-as-rocks medical examiner.

"I can't tell you that you're wrong," Lilah said, in a small voice. "But I can't tell you you're right either. Even if I knew for sure, how would we put it on the record?" The doctor searched Lilah's eyes.

"Okay, hypothetically then," she started "If it were a vampire, just suppose, would John Doe rise again?" Since they were talking in the hypothetical, Lilah could answer her.

"No," She shook head slightly, "From what I know, from books and legends, he would have had to have been killed by the vampire, and right before his heart stopped, shared blood with the same vampire who bit him. This man died of strangulation. If, and only if they existed, which we know they don't, they didn't want him to rise. I suspect he was food." Or even a feast, though one set of marks implied only one vampire.

"So hypothetically, we don't have to stake him," Dr. Collins smiled, but it didn't reach her eyes. She knew, but didn't want to completely believe. Lilah didn't blame her.

"No, we don't. Leave it off the record doctor. We know how he was killed. Perhaps those were flea or mosquito bites." The doctor nodded.

"If asked, that is exactly what they are." Lilah stood.

"I've got to go Dr. Thank you. If anything more comes up, let me know." It was a code they both knew well. It didn't have to be Lilah's case, but if something came in that just wasn't normal, Doctor Collins would call her first. She always had, and until now, Lilah had perfectly rational explanations.

"I'll call Lilah. You know damn well I will! His manner of death will be marked strangulation, aided by exsanguination caused by trauma to the femoral artery. Because any one else looking can find the wound, however, the rest stays between us". Dr. Collins wasn't one much for swearing , because she was so proper. Yet she said 'Damn' twice tonight.

the doctor for the rest of her life. If the doctor was lucky, it would be only the memories that hurt. If any other vampires found out she knew they existed, Dr. Dru might be next on that slab. Lilah was afraid that someday soon, they'd need to have "the talk." She hoped it was later, much later.

As Lilah left the hospital, the sky was already the blue of the color of the ocean as the sun sets. They'd been talking for over two hours. It was now well past 8pm, and Lilah still had the club to check out, but first she had to make a call. Pulling out her cell, she hit the quick dial to her department at the SPD.

"Burton, Chief Dave Burton," Lilah's boss always answered his phone like that. It's strange, but it seemed like most police and military people do.

"Hey Dave, its Lilah. I just wanted to check in, and let you know I'm following a lead." Lilah could feel the sigh before he let it out.

"What about your partner?"

"Dave, this is nothing big, and could potentially waste time needed to find out about John Doe. If the lead pans out, I'll call him in."

"Lieutenant Evans, I know that you and partners don't always get along well, but if you find anything, I expect it all to be shared with Detective Davies, is that clear?"

"Yes sir." There was nothing else she could say. An order, is an order. She'd worked too long to get where she was to blow it by being rude to her superior officer.

"See that you do. Report in, if anything comes up." He hung up. Lilah read that police were like that, at least here in the Colonies. It was different in other parts of the world. She put the phone back, and headed toward Ravens. She chose to walk, not wanting to risk running into Davies by retrieving her car from the station. Not yet, anyway, and it was only about 15 blocks. Nothing more than a brisk walk in the night air to someone like Lilah.

The city is so alive at night; the air itself tugs this way and that. There is an energy in Seattle that she'd felt nowhere else, and Lilah speculated that it was magic. Lilah had met enough people, to know those with "gifts" were drawn here, and drawn to each other. She'd felt it herself, but stayed away from the places of the greatest magic. It wouldn't do if anyone learned her secret, and magic scared her. Like the night, it flirted with her, tempting her with power. She was afraid she'd lose her humanity.

Still, when the night called, Lilah wanted to take it, and pull it though her fingers like dark salt-water taffy. To taste it, or drink it up, and hold onto the energy, or power, which she knew would open other things for her. Things Lilah's father had helped her lock tight inside. As much as she wanted it, Lilah was too afraid to take the chance. While feeling the air around her, she nearly walked passed the club.

Not that it tried to hide itself. A red and black neon sign stood out from the door. Red was the background color, too bright to be blood, too dark to mean anything else. In black, two ravens circled each other, as though they'd dropped through the air, though never touching, facing each other for all eternity.

As Lilah reached for the door, a large man, with a grey beard and pony tail blocked her way.

"Ma'am I'm sorry, but we aren't letting people in yet." Lilah was pretty sure some VIP's had been let in. Didn't matter though, she had her own ticket.

Lilah pulled out her badge, and held it up, "Seattle PD, I just need to come in and take a look around." She smiled, and tried to look pretty and harmless, like "Hey, just doing my job." The bouncer stared for a moment, trying to decide if it was worth the fight to keep her out. Good judgment won. Or maybe he'd seen the insides of one too many jail cells. He pulled back that mighty velvet rope, and even bowed slightly as Lilah walked through the door. That struck her as somewhat odd, but she shrugged as she went inside.

Once through the door, noise smacked Lilah in the face, and had she been human might have caused her to stumble. The bouncer said he wasn't letting anyone in, so it was awfully crowded for no one. Lilah wasn't sure how people could communicate through this kind of din, but it did give her a good bit of cover. She was another woman, looking for a good time, if you didn't see the gun and the badge.

Lilah made her way to the bar, and found one stool unoccupied. The night was still young, and people were trying to enjoy every second of it. For many, night equals freedom. Lilah ordered a beer she never planned to touch. It was all part of the disguise and she hated the taste of beer.

Once settled, Lilah shut her eyes, getting a feel for the room, and the different energies of each person. They'd never know that she'd touched them in a way more intimate than most lovers. More importantly, Lilah would have a better idea of who and what she was dealing with. It was when she reached the second floor dance area that she found something. Power licked through the room, picking up the pieces left behind by those who didn't understand their own energy. It fed from them, just as taking human blood would, only not as strong.

Lilah hadn't felt that kind of power in 200 years, not since her father had left her alone, fearing for her life. Most vampires stayed out of cities, preferring the seclusion, and relative safety of the country. In fact, there were very few that Lilah knew of in the States. Yet, there were at least four different vampires up there, dancing. It was that power that called to Lilah, which showed them to her.

Not knowing if her power called to them, and gave her away, Lilah made it slowly to the stairs, to meet with them. Fear almost kept her from going. Lilah's father always told her if "full" vampires found her, she'd be killed. On the other hand, just as she could feel them, and it called to her, like a spell cast in the night. She hoped possible that whatever powers gave her that ability to feel them, shielded her from their own "vampdar." If so, Lilah was safe for another night.

It was less crowed up here, only about 15 or so people, most sitting at small tables, talking, but a few danced.

Looking around, Lilah first tried to use her eyes to detect any threats. Lilah couldn't tell without walking up to one and saying "Hey, can I see your eyes?" That might be a bit too obvious, plus she was afraid they'd see through her. Instead, she shut her eyes again, seeing in her head where everyone was standing or sitting. Power blazed from a couple at one of the tables, and nearly blinded her from the dance floor. Lilah had to grab the railing to keep from falling backwards, the power flash made her weak. She must have swayed slightly

"Madam, are you okay?" It was a British accent, a voice Lilah didn't recognize. She didn't feel power from the man in front of her, and decided it was safe to open her eyes. His voice seemed to have broken the spell. She no longer felt pulled to the vampires.

"It's Lieutenant, thank you. I must have missed my step."

Long blond hair was pulled back into a leather tie; bright, golden eyes, a color she'd seen on no one else, searched Lilah's for a sign that she was telling the truth, about either being all right, or being police. For a moment, just looking at him made her nearly speechless, as he was so beautiful and so very human. Lilah's training, years of dealing with people, and beautiful men, kept her from drooling. Just. She grasped the outstretched hand and steadied herself.

"Thank you though, for your help..."

"Liam Campbell."

The last name was definitely Scottish, the first Irish. Lilah felt at a loss, but let it go. She had a job to do, and she hoped man would have something to say about the bar. Maybe drop a clue, or seven.

"How often do you come in here, Mr. Campbell? If you have a moment..."

"Lieutenant, if I'm to be interrogated can we at least sit down? And give me a name, first, please." His smile said it was a joke, but his eyes had gone hard, cold. He didn't like having the police ask him questions.

"We can do that. Downstairs," Lilah wanted as far away from the power she'd felt as possible. If they had noticed her presence, they'd done nothing to show it.

Liam Campbell did better than a regular booth downstairs, he had an office. Lilah didn't realize he was the owner, and felt like a fool for not to having looked it up. This was for a friend, she told herself, trying to excuse her lack of due diligence.

He showed her to leather backed, stiff looking chair, before he set himself behind the desk. It was obviously his place of power, where he felt secure, and Lilah was sure, safe from the police.

"How may I help you, Lieutenant?" His accent was clipped, angry.

Lilah was silent for a moment, contemplating. Did she bring up John Doe? Did she bring up Cris' missing friend, Lisa? Lilah thought it best to avoid the vampires.

"I'm here investigating two things Mr. Campbell. The first is the disappearance of a young college student. She was last seen dancing here, with another of your clientele. Her best friends couldn't get her to come away with them. Her name is Lisa James. She hasn't called, showed up for class, nor was she seen after her friends decided to leave the club." Lilah produced a picture of the three girls Cris had given her a while back, to prove she was making legitimate friends.

"Do any of these girls look familiar?" Lilah wanted to see his eyes on a cold read, before she pointed to the girl that was missing.

Liam picked up the picture and seemed to be studying it seriously for several moments. He then swore in a Romani, a language Lilah knew the odd word of, but was anything but fluent. Handing the picture back to Lilah, he shook his head slightly.

"I saw all three of them in here last night. And you're correct, I only saw two of them leave. Perhaps it's just a one night dalliance?" His face said he thought differently, and Lilah could hear his heart beat just a little bit faster.

"Mr. Campbell, lying to the cops can carry a heavy penalty, and I happen to know you are lying. Try again!" Lilah was more than a little perturbed. She pointed to the girl on the right in the picture "This is Lisa. If you thought this was a one night stand, why would you have cursed upon looking at this picture?"

Liam paled a little, and met her eyes.

"You speak Romani?"

"Not fluently, but everyone knows swearing when they hear it!"

"You are not what you seem, are you Lieutenant."

"Are you?" It was a strange small bit of banter, and Lilah was sure she was correct. Liam Campbell was no mild mannered club owner. He fooled her back in the bar itself, when she was sure he was human. Now, she was pretty sure he wasn't. He met Lilah's eyes, and seemed surprised as what he found there. Or what he didn't.

"I think, we should level with each other."

"About what?" Lilah wasn't about to admit to being half-vampire.

"How about, being more than we seem? Would that work for you?"

"Fine. Now, back to the girls?" Lilah sighed.

"Fine then. We agree. Now, to the missing girl, as I assume the other two made it home safely?"

"Yes."

"I saw her." He gave an exasperated sigh, "she was dancing with Viggo Turov." Liam stopped there, watching Lilah's face. She felt a chill run through her already cooler body temperature. Turov was a name her father had used often. Usually with the words "stay away from". She knew there were vampires here, but if a Turov was one of them, she shouldn't be. Yet, she couldn't let Cris down, and she had to follow up on John Doe as well.

"Do you have any idea where they went?" Lilah tried to keep her fear to herself, but could see in Liam's eyes that he knew.

"No. They left with Viggo's man, Dimitri." Lilah had a sinking feeling her cases just became one.

"Mr. Campbell..."

"Liam, please."

"Liam, have you seen this man." I slid the John Doe picture across the desk. Liam's heart rate sped again. But this time he didn't swear.

"Yes. That is Dimitri." Interesting, the implication made Dimitri a human servant to one bad-ass vampire. And now, he was dead, by vampiric hands. Lilah's case just fell into the "cold case" category fairly quickly. Except for one thing: the ligature marks.

"Liam, what can you tell me about Viggo and Dimitri. And level with me, do you think Lisa James is actually still alive. "

"Lieutenant..."

"Lilah, please. Unless we're around other cops. "

Liam smiled then, and it wasn't unpleasant or forced. Just for a moment, Lilah found herself compelled by how beautiful he really was. Until he laughed.

"I wondered if that worked on one such as you."

"What?"

"Glamor. I promise, Lilah. Some day you and I will sit down, and we'll talk about it all. Until then, I shall not do that again.

"Do I believe Lisa James is still alive?" He switched topics, leaving Lilah's head spinning. It'd be a cold day in hell before she spilled her secrets to him.

"Honestly Lilah, I do not know. I would not have expected anything to happen to Dimitri. Perhaps, Turov has chosen a new...companion." The word fell with distaste from Liam's lips, making Lilah feel a little better. She had no desire to fall in with someone who loved the worst of the worst.

"And Viggo is gone. He was here for one night, he said. Thought he felt something in Seattle that needed taking care of. When he left last night, he said he was mistaken, and that he was leaving for Europe again. I'm afraid he took Ms. James with him."

So was Lilah. This wasn't the news she wanted to bring back to Cris. And how was she going to deal with John Doe's death? It was a case she couldn't solve, without outing herself. And she was not crazy enough to do that. She stood to leave, putting her hand out to shake Liam's hand.

"Thank you Mr...Liam. All useful information, none of which I can use as a cop. And this is a letdown for Lisa's friends and family. All I can tell them is...that she's gone, and there are no clues. This is not a great day for Law Enforcement in Seattle."

"It's not as bleak as you may think, Lilah. Trust me."

"Thank you again."

"I hope we meet again, very soon." That happy lilt to his accent was back, as he was no longer addressing the police, but Lilah herself. She nodded, but did not echo his sentiments. She didn't want to learn more secrets. He shook her hand, and raised an eyebrow slightly, but said nothing more.

Lilah left quickly, trying not to get the attention of the powerful vampires that were still in the bar, and hit the streets. The night smelled like all nights: dark and brassy always with a hint of salt and blood. For the first time since walking into the club, she felt safe again. Even if it was a false sense of safe, Lilah knew the night was where she belonged. She made her way to the precinct, as promised to pick up her new "partner" and not solve John Doe's murder.

When Lilah got to her floor, it was louder than she expected.

"Well, if it isn't the prodigy on solving crimes!" Crap, Davies was already there, and sill obnoxious.

"Nice to see you too Davies. Been working hard?" He sneered at her.

"Actually yes, partner," sarcasm at its best "while you were out 'chasing down leads' I caught John Doe's killer." He sneered at her. Lilah must have looked surprised for a moment, which Davies noticed.

"You're speechless, I love it! Come meet the killer. He's in interrogation. Getting ready to spill his guts. Name is Erik Branter." Lilah followed Davies, weaving around detective's desks, until reaching the bare, bleak interrogation rooms. She was anxious to learn who'd copped to a murder they didn't commit. Stopping to the look through the one way glass, she took a sharp intake of breath. It was the bouncer who didn't want to let her into Ravens. He was a big, strong man to be sure. But, he was human. Lilah knew he was human from the moment she'd met him. While she watched, he wrote quickly on the paper in front of him.

"He's writing his confession already?"

"Mr. Branter came in a few hours ago, demanding to speak to you. When I said you weren't here, that I was your partner, he was willing to talk to me. The first thing out of his mouth was 'a present from Turov'. I couldn't get him to explain it, and he seemed to have forgotten what he said. But he remembers the murder. He choked and beat up our John Doe, whose name is Dimitri. Branter doesn't know his last name. He even admitted to leaving him in that alley to die." Davies seemed so pleased with himself, that Lilah couldn't help but take him down, just a peg.

"So the great murder mystery, that you solved, walked itself in here, and admitted to it. Asking for me? I admire your skills Detective. I wish I was half the Detective you are. Really, you must teach me that trick some time." Sarcasm also helped mask the utter terror Lilah was feeling. If Turov sent Branter to her, there was a good chance he knew her secret.

"Laugh all you want, but the case is closing, without you doing anything!" He sobered from the banter for a moment "Let's look at it this way. One more bad guy off the streets, right?"

"I did nothing? I was chasing down a lead. You were sitting in the police station. I'd met Branter once. He gave off none of the signals of a killer." She took a deep breath, "goes to show, you can't always win. So yes, good that another bad guy is off the streets." It wasn't true, and the cop in her ached. This wasn't justice, it was a tragedy.

Lilah walked into the room with Davies and read over the confession. Lilah also saw Branter's eyes, dull and lost. He was under the thrall of a vampire, Turov to be exact. The confession was perfect. It closed the case, but a bad taste in Lilah's mouth, having to put an innocent man in jail.

Turning to Davies "Good job," was all she said as she left the room. She had to call Cris, and then, maybe just go home. Feign a headache. Cris cried, when Lilah said she found nothing, and that the trail was too cold to follow. Lilah warned Cris against ever going to Ravens again.

The worst part of it all, it wasn't over. The owner of Ravens knew Lilah was supernatural, as was he. Viggo Turov had sent this man to her, not Davies, to clear up this murder, and she had a feeling nothing was over. The vampires knew she existed, and there would be a reckoning. She hoped it would be a long time coming.

The sun was beginning to edge over the horizon, as she finished her paperwork and headed home. For today, Lilah was safe.

Chapter One

The Puget Sound was choppy, dark, and soothing. The wind whipped the waves, sending sprays of dark blue water cascading over the random ferries, piers and any people out late enough to be caught in the weather. Homicide Lieutenant Lilah Evans was spending one of her rare nights off, staring out at the dark water and believing she can see the inlet to the ocean, and beyond. The wind played with her with her dark, raven locks of hair, like a tired, casual lover not caring which direction it went, and tangling it as they go. Lilah didn't care; it was nights like this she was homesick and missed her father. Vampire or not, he was the only family she had.

Lilah shook her head as another spray of water burst over her head, covering her in light droplets of salt water. Her soft, brown leather bomber jacked saturated in the wind and rain, but Lilah didn't care. She couldn't feel the cold anyway. The sliver of the moon gave off nearly no light, but this wasn't a problem for Lilah. She understood the dark, which exploded around her, awash with colors no one else could see. Brilliant blues, emerald greens, and deep amethyst purple. The night offered protection, with a hint of temptation. That protection kept her safe from the other things that go bump in the night. Or perhaps boom, depending on the situation.

Night Hues

This wasn't Lilah's first time on the pier, longing for Europe, but it was different. Now, she held fear in her heart. After all, the last time she sat here, she wasn't being pursued by an ancient and powerful vampire: Viggo Turov.

Lilah had never met Turov in person. Somehow he knew about her. She worked a case involving the nightclub Ravens several months before. The bastard baited her: first with a dead body, then with a missing girl. Viggo Turov was so evil, he enthralled the bouncer from the nightclub to say he, Eric Branter, had murdered the man in the alley. A man who, in fact had been Turov's companion for decades, if not longer. Lastly, he'd had Branter say that he was a "present from Turov" for Lilah. All in all, it chilled Lilah down to her bones. He had to know her secret, and that lost her safety and anonymity. Though months had passed without sign of Turov, he was on Lilah's mind.

Sighing, breathing in the mist and salt from the water of the night, Lilah stood. She'd decided Turov was a problem for another day, and she couldn't stay on the pier forever. Maybe she'd stop at Ravens, as the owner intrigued her, on a personal level. Or head home. Sleep for a change. Stronger than human, with more stamina, Lilah still needed to sleep. It was a safe place in a world full of monsters. "Vampires," on average tended to lose anything that once made them human, including the ability to procreate though sex. Vampirism is a parasite of the soul. A human catches it from a bite, and they die. Well, the body doesn't, but it darkens and devours their humanity. They may still walk, and talk, but for the rest of eternity they are missing that which made them human. It was also why they couldn't find themselves in reflective surfaces. There was nothing left inside to reflect. Lilah Evangeline Evans was something else. She could see all but her eyes in a mirror, proof that she both had the parasite, and her humanity.

Add heightened senses, strength, agility and speed didn't hurt either. The ability to smell the blood in the rain, helped make her a good cop. Lilah was told other "powers" could happen over time. She wasn't holding her breath.

But that's where the good stopped. Lilah couldn't enthrall humans, had very little magic, and though she could feel the night, she couldn't use it to her advantage, as she was pretty sure it would pull more of her soul towards the monster she didn't want to be. It wasn't all bad though, as Lilah was approaching her third century and looked like a human of 26. Though she didn't believe she'd live forever, she was fairly sure it was going to be close enough. Once, in a pique of fatherly love, Lilah was told that there had been one other like her. Sadly, she'd been burned at the stake in medieval Europe, and there were no records. She was a mystery or a myth. Lilah always wondered if her father had made up the strange other "part human" just to make her feel better.

Lilah's mother died when she was still little, being human as she was. Her father stayed as long as he could. But Lilah was taboo, a secret. Sovampire politics called him away. Baron Ricard Von Easton would be one of the monsters, if it kept his little girl safe. He'd always told her that she was a threat to "normal" vampires. For some reason, perhaps it was love, her father chose to stay away, rather than have them learn of Lilah. To the rest of the world, vampires, lycanthropes, and many other things were nothing but legend. Lilah knew it was all real. Evil, good, something in between; it all existed. And it was a reality throughout the world, and in modern day Seattle. Lilah hadn't run into many other supernatural beings in Seattle, but she knew they could be there, away from her reach. Which was exactly why she'd become a homicide cop.

It didn't matter that the night called to her, a lullaby she couldn't block out, nor could she embrace it fully, and stay who she was. And who she was, mattered to Lilah. It kept her alive, compassionate, loving and most of all, nearly human. All of which, made her a good homicide Lieutenant.

Turning to leave, having decided on a drink at Ravens, a familiar odor floated in on the Puget Sound winds. Dark, cloying and sickly sweet, it was as familiar as an old friend, and as horrible as every nightmare. The smell of decaying flesh, mixed with briny decay that water held in its darker depths. Lilah knew it well, a sense memory that would never fade, vampire or human. Following her nose, she ended up partly under the pier as the tide slowly rolled out, uncovering a body. One look told her it was homicide, and just like that, she was on the job. Shaking her head, she pulled out her cell phone and called the station.

"Homicide".

"This is Lieutenant Lilah Evans; I'm down on the waterfront, off of and partially under pier 70, at the foot of Clay and Broad Street. I've encountered a body, that looks like a homicide. Please call in Detective Allen Davies, the ME on call, and forensics. Let's get the gang together. Have them meet me here."

Dispatch answered in the affirmative and Lilah hung up. It was a bad habit she'd gotten into since becoming a cop, not saying good-bye. Or maybe she'd said it too many times, and was tired of good-byes, even temporary ones. While she waited, she observed the body without touching it.

The body was female, and she'd been in the water at least 48 hours, possibly longer. Her face was unrecognizable. She'd been shot at close range in the face, possibly with a sawed off shot-gun and buckshot. That was for the Medical

Examiner to determine. The killer probably intended to erase the victim, make her not "be" any longer. Usually due to rage, but rage is not necessarily the only reason to do this type of damage. If they were worried about the body being identified, they slipped up badly. The corpse still had her hands and feet intact, though obviously nibbled on by fish, and would likely yield fingerprints. If anyone could do it, she knew it was her Medical Examiner: Doctor Drusilla Collins.

Lilah found herself annoyed. It had been such a nice night. Whomever it was that ruined her night was going to have a bad time when she found them. It wasn't just that her day off was ruined. Lilah hated to see the waste of human life, whether it be the woman in front of her, or the animal that killed her. Both had thrown whatever life they had away. Something Lilah would make sure of in the latter case. Being half-vampire gave Lilah a unique perspective of the value of human life. Full vampires saw human as pets at best, cattle at worst. They didn't have value other than entertainment or food. It was what the human could do for the vampire. Lilah didn't eat "Long Pig," which was what the Maori had called "human." She believed that a human life sacred. Not to a god, or demon, but to that person, to the earth, to something intangible. It really pissed her off to see it go to waste.

Lilah shook her head as she heard the sirens in the distance. Her people were coming, and this woman was now going to get treated in death like she hadn't in life. She was going to matter, and be important to several people. Sometimes, that was the best they could do.

Chapter Two

"Should I assume you got here and found the body, or did you just bring one with you?" Detective Allen Davies stood near Lilah, the body still in the shallows as they did their examination of the scene. The night was turning from the inky black of midnight to the deep blue of the sea, always the calm before the storm. Lieutenant Lilah Evans had a few more hours before she'd have to seek shelter.

"You're a real comedian, Davies. Maybe you followed the wrong career?"

"Har de Har," Lilah hadn't heard that since the 1960's. It sounded odd coming out of Allen's mouth. "Seriously, how'd you find this one?"

"Either good luck, or someone else's really bad luck. I was walking home after being out with some friends," she lied "and heard something splashing around. Curiosity got the best me, as usual." Lilah lied, because some things, like her days off, were personal. Nothing she did before finding the body affected the case, so she felt justified.

"So Detective Davies, this time, *you* dazzle *me*." When they'd first been assigned to work together, Allen Davies had been like several other police officers who felt Lilah was weird for working nights, for requesting/finding and solving the freaky cases. She had a reputation as a weirdo and a hotshot, combinations few other cops wanted to work with. When Davies met Lilah, he didn't want to work with her either. Though she had rank, he believed he had experience, and didn't want to be shown up. So the first thing he said, on that case was "Dazzle me". The problem was that she did. Detective Allen Davies still spared with her, and joked with her in public or squad room, but unlike other partner's she'd had in the past, he didn't ask for a transfer. Five months later, they may actually enjoy each other's company.

"The victim seems to be Caucasian, though it's hard to tell with the water damage and the nibbles that have been taken. Female, hands and feet intact, again except for what the fish have eaten... face is nearly non-existent, though I can make out an eye socket. On first glance, she was shot with something at close range and then thrown into Puget Sound. Which is an overused cliché." Davies wasn't wrong there. Throwing a body in the water was old school. Without weights, the body was easy to find. Gases make a corpse buoyant, and they come floating to the surface.

"What if it wasn't a stupid move to throw her in the Sound? What if, we're supposed to think it's a rookie mistake?" Lilah mused aloud.

"Why the hell would someone do that? Seems like a lot of work to me," Detective Davies sneered.

"I don't know Davies. It was a thought, just one theory to keep in mind while we investigate." Although the she'd voiced the idea, it didn't feel right. Lilah was afraid it was something far more sinister.

Lilah was glad to hear the Medical Examiner van pull up, onto the pebbles by the pier. If more answers were to be found, it would be their job. Due to the corpse's time in the water, Lilah couldn't track anything by smell, and feeling the body right now would compromise the already fragile skin.

When the head medical examiner, Doctor Drusilla Collins got out of the van herself, Lilah was relieved. Everyone at the Police Department/Seattle General Hospital morgue were good, but the director herself? She was better. Dru smiled at Lilah while getting out of the van, hers white teeth a contrast to her dark skin, and the cerulean of the night. They shared a secret, the cop and the doctor. They only spoke of it once; the case Lilah worked that involved Viggo Turov. But Doctor Drusilla Collins suspected that some of the things in the dark of nightmares really existed. One can only be blind to the strange deaths in Seattle for so long.

"Floater, eh?" the doctor asked.

"Yup, and it looks like a nasty way to go. I'd bet you that this is a homicide. Take a look." As the good doctors assistants were making their way down the shore, Dru took a moment to look over the body. She shook her head sadly.

"You're right about that. It's not suicide. There's way more than meets the eye here, but this poor lady did not shoot *herself* in the face. If in fact, the gunshot was her cause of death. We'll know more when we get her back to the morgue. Donovan, Reece, get your butts in gear. I think this woman has been in the water long enough." Dru called to her assistants.

"Yes ma'am" Donovan said with a smirk. It wasn't derision or insubordination. Every time Lilah had seen twenty-five year old, pale blond ME's assistant, he always had a smirk. Reece was new, so Lilah hadn't met him before. He was a stark contrast to Donovan, with dark hair and brooding eyes. She noticed Reece gave Donovan a dirty look, which he quickly shielded to no reaction before looking at the body. It was obvious to Lilah that the new guy didn't like Donovan very much. Which was strange. Everyone, even Detective Davies, liked Donovan.

'Don't ma'am me, Don, I'm not that old." Dru always said that, and it was mostly true. At least, she couldn't have been his mother. But she always said it with a smile, maybe it answered the smirk. Either way, they got on very well.

"You guys got this?" inquired Lilah. The sky had changed from cerulean and was now the beginnings of purple and pink of the morning light. "I need to go file a report".

"Go, both of you. She's mine now. I'll let you know what I find." With that, Lilah and Davies were excused from the crime scene. Since Lilah didn't have a car, she rode with Davies back to the Seattle Police Department, main office, just as the sun was peeking over Capitol Hill.

Chapter Three

Lilah walked into the squad room, and noticed Officers Harper and Frye struggling with a man in cuffs, an overcoat and not much else. He was standing, struggling against both of them, trying to spit and kick. Lilah rushed over and pushed him back into the bench. Her strength made him sit quickly, and he looked slightly stunned as to how he got there. He looked at her, and made a rude gesture, even in the cuffs. She shook her head.

"Officers, is there a reason you didn't have this man under control? There are two of you, and one of him. Need classes in restraint? Some time on traffic duty?"

"No sir," Frye answered immediately. He was fairly new to the squad, and like many who only knew Lilah by reputation, was a bit afraid of her. Plus she had rank. But Daisy Harper smirked a bit. She'd been with the SPD a while, and had transferred to homicide not that long ago.

"Sorry Lieutenant." Harper meant the words, but always had a hint of humor in her voice. "This is Barney Linner, or so his ID says. We found him standing over a body in Pioneer Square, shouting nonsense. No idea if he was involved or if there was even a crime, but he was at least drunk and disorderly. Trying to interview him, we immediately noticed another problem. He's on...something. And we can't pin it down. Seems to give him extra strength, he wanted to fight as soon as he saw us. I have no idea if the asshole part is just his personality."

Lilah nodded slightly toward Harper, then leaned down, trying to ignore the body odor and sweat, pretending she was looking him in the eyes. Instead, she was smelling him for drugs. There was something there, acrid, nearly acidic, strong and slightly sweet. She'd never smelled it before. But it was his eyes that weren't right. Lilah assumed it was a trick of the light, but they seem to subtly change colors as she looked. Just as she was about to stand back up, he leaned over and whispered "I see you...don't think I can't see what you are." Linner then sat back in silence.

"I think Mr. Linner is going to agree to a drug test. Once you get the results call me. Also, get in touch with the ME about the body you found. We need to know if this is a homicide case, a Vice case or if we have to bump it to someone else." Lilah started to walk to her office, and turned back "And if I find you two with a suspect uncontrolled again, it's going to be a few days of nothing but scut work." She grinned, and made her way to her office. Maybe she was a little scary.

Lilah's office was in the back of the bullpen. It had a tiny window, which she'd covered with a "re-creation" of Vincent Van Gogh's *Starry Night*. Lilah had really liked Van Gogh, and often wished he'd been alive when mental health services were available. They'd only met a few times, but they'd made an impression on each other. Enough so, that he'd given her the painting she adored the most. It was an amazing interpretation of the night, and it kept the sunlight out. Lilah sat down and sighed. Death was a part of human life, but some were so needless. Like Van Gogh's, or the woman in the morgue. Maybe even the body Linner was standing over. Shaking her head, she reached over, and flipped on her monitor. Time to write her report.

A few hours later, the report was typed and sent to the Captain's computer. Lilah's head was splitting, and she wasn't looking forward to finding her way home during the day. She could do it of course, as the Seattle Police Department's garage had two floors under it that most people didn't know about. Sewer access which lead to access to Underground Seattle. Lilah had studied Seattle seriously while she was considering making her second trip to the Pacific North West, and did enough reconnaissance work to find that everywhere she normally needed to go in the city: her apartment, the morgue, and SPD were all connected by one of the two sets of tunnels, mostly unused. They were dangerous to the average tourist, but Lilah was no tourist. She avoided the used parts of the Seattle Underground. So really, the trip home wasn't the problem. The real problem was that she was hungry, which didn't help the headache at all. But the steak Lilah had waiting in her small apartment? It would help immensely. Human pain killers, for the most part, had no effect on Lilah. Though she was half human, she metabolized things at a different rate.

Smiling, Lilah flipped her computer monitor back off, and shrugged into her black trench coat. It had been a long day already, and she feared what was coming next from the medical examiner. Home and rest seemed the best bet, for now. Leaving her office, and locking it as she did, she looked around the bullpen. These were her people, and this was where she belonged. Even the smells were right: sweat, sugar, coffee, with an undertone of piss. Exactly what a bullpen should smell like.

"Well, night guys." She smiled at the three people in the pen. Frye, Harper and Davies.

"It's 9am," observed Frye.

"Yup, bedtime. The nightshift changes perspective."

"I'm with you Evans'. Heading home myself, need a lift?" Davies asked.

"I have my own way. See you on the flip side." Lilah laughed a little at her own dated joke, and quickly left. She didn't need anyone watching how she left the building. Lilah was able to use her speed on her way to the sewer access, to avoid being seen by the other Officers. Once there, she descended to the tunnels below.

Chapter Four

Though she was underground, Lilah could feel the day beating at her, a reminder that she's other. It pulled and pushed at her different sides, human toward the sun and vampire further into the darkness, increasing her headache. She sighed as the door to her apartment building came into sight. Once more she had to go a floor up, but she was still in her thankfully dark and cool apartment building. She made the stairs in less than a second, and slammed her door as she nearly leaped into her own home. Food and bed never looked so inviting.

Lilah grabbed her cast iron pan, and put it on the stove. She quickly unwrapped on of the extra bloody steaks she kept in her refrigerator, and tossed it into the pan. A quick sear on one side, a flip and for her, and it was perfect. A nice, even char on the outside, and blue rare on the inside. Lilah didn't drink blood, human or animal, but she still required a large source of iron, and steak rare was the quickest and tastiest way. To be truthful, she'd never tried blood straight. Lilah didn't want to tempt her dark side, or lose any more of her soul.

After dinner, Lilah took stock of herself in the bathroom mirror. As usual, she couldn't see her eyes, but all else was visible. Vampirism isn't what people read about in fiction stories or weird sparkly movies. It was dark, dangerous, and evil. Lilah feared the day she looked into a mirror and saw nothing gazing back. Which is why she shied away from blood itself, from the other kinds of magic that pull at her in the dark. They'd make her even faster, stronger, and more powerful than she could imagine, but Lilah was sure, if she gave in, it would consume her soul.

Turning away, Lilah shed her clothes and nearly fell into bed. Her day off had turned into something much busier, and she was tired. Even vampires need sleep. She was asleep before her head hit the pillow.

It was dark. So dark, yet Lilah could hear someone calling her name. She turned every direction, but the darkness didn't lift.

"Who's there?"

"Lilah…" again her name floated in, though there was no wind.

"What do you want?"

"Daughter…"

"Sir? Father? Where are we?" She felt lost, hearing the voice from her past. Lilah had not heard from him in a century or so.

"The only safe place for us to talk, my child. The ether. Your dreams, if you like."

Lilah rarely dreamed, and never about her father.

"Father, it's been so long…"

"It's the only way to keep you safe. Though I fear even this will not work anymore. You've been found, dear child. If one vampire knows, it's only a matter of time before other's find out. Which puts you in mortal danger."

"I know. I don't know how Viggo Turov found me out. So far, he hasn't returned to hurt me. But I know he's dangerous."

"That is not your only foe, daughter. Watch for the colors. There is something new in the night that threatens us all."

"What father? Please..."

"That's all I know, my dear. Stay safe. You are what anchors me to this world. The only person that keeps even a shred of my humanity intact. So be careful."

"Yes sir." Years of conditioning had her answering him such. She grew up in a time, where you respected all elders, or you got whipped. And this, her father, was one elder she always respected.

"Good." Baron Ricard Von Easton never said he loved her, he came from a time where it was not necessary. But he kept her safe by staying in that in the world of evil, by being the monster he never wanted her to be. To her, that was all the "I love you" she needed. He said nothing more, and the darkness faded: the voice was gone. She was alone.

She woke with a start, in a dark room as always. Lilah couldn't shake the "conversation" she'd had with her father. Was he really there, did the Baron come to her in her dreams? It felt very real, but it was also new. Her father had never come to her like that in the past. It was unsettling, comforting and informative. Lilah knew now that while Turov was a threat, there was something new out there.

Watch for the colors...

What in the nine hells did that mean? Did he mean actual lights? The sun? Something else? Something niggled at the back of her thoughts, but she couldn't place it. Lilah realized she'd have to stay on guard. Which really wasn't new, as Lilah felt she was always hyper-vigilant. So when the phone rang, Lilah only jumped slightly. Yup, hyper-vigilant.

"Evans"

"Lilah? This is Doctor Collins. I need you to come to the morgue." Lilah could hear the desperation in her voice. Not much, just a tinge, a human probably wouldn't even notice. Lilah took it as a deep disturbance.

"What time is it?" Everyone knew Lilah worked nights, and it was possible Dru was beginning to suspect why. They danced around the subject but they never outright spoke of it.

"6pm. Can you get here?" Lilah'd slept longer than she thought. With the tunnel access and the sun going down, she'd be able to get there in no time.

"I'll be there shortly."

"Good." They hung up, no pleasantries. It seemed to go with the territory.

Chapter Five

Lilah headed out. Since the sun hadn't completely set yet, she used the basement exit. It was free of windows and only had the exit to the Underground. Lilah moved quickly, faster than human speed, taking no more than ten minutes to get the six miles to Seattle General, the hospital that housed all of Seattle's homicides. It's amazing how many places in this city had lower levels. Luckily for Lilah, Seattle General was one of them. It had been built in the '50's, made to withstand fire, and even the occasional earthquake. It also had underground sewer access, which was meant to be a bomb shelter as well. At the end of her journey into the hospital, there was an old, rusted iron door. She'd long ago torn off the padlock, but always put it back in place. This area was unused, and the door was ignored by the staff. Lilah didn't think they even saw it anymore.

After a quick listen to be sure the hallway was clear, Lilah moved passed the door, and into the hospital proper. She straightened her black trench coat, making sure it covered her shoulder holster carrying her Sig Saur 911. Lilah didn't want to freak anyone in the hospital out by accidently flashing the firearm. Once she was sure it was situated, Lilah made her way to Dr. Dru's office, which was connected to the morgue by a door. Last time Lilah visited Dru was dictating into a hand held tape recorder. This time she was sitting with her head in her hands staring at the computer.

Doctor Drusilla Collins was a tall women when she stood, around 6 foot with strikingly deep brown eyes, skin the color of a good dark chocolate, often with purple highlights in the right light. She kept her dark hair cut short, straightened and always well-coiffed.

"Doctor Collins?" The Medical Examiner looked up with a start. She'd been lost in her own thoughts.

"Oh Lilah. I'm rather glad to see you. I'm at a loss on this one." Dru sighed "What did you think at the crime scene today? About the cause of death?"

"Well, we both assumed it was a gunshot of some kind, though I admit, I haven't seen one do that kind of damage before."

"Nor had I," answered Dru, "though it was theoretically possible. But I've since searched the body for the bullets, pellets, or whatever else could be fired from a gun. There isn't anything there. No trace of metal, except for, what I'm pretty sure was a gold hoop in her right ear. The other ear was eaten by the wildlife in the Sound." Never one to pull punches, Doctor Dru.

"Could the metal have been washed away by the tide?"

"Not all of it, it's just not possible. Those wounds were deep and there would have been, at the very least, a fragment stuck in her skull. I did send a few swabs off to the lab, looking for traces, being thorough and all. But I have a hunch we won't be finding any." Doctor Dru was perplexed. This case shouldn't be so complicated, at least not on her end. Instead, it was starting to give her a headache.

Lilah looked at the good doctor for a moment and shook her head.

"I can take another look. You might want to stay here." Lilah left unspoken the truth: Drusilla Collins probably didn't want to know all her secrets. After all, denial is a state of being, not a river in Egypt. Just for a moment, Drusilla looked like she wanted to come, to question what Lilah was going do to her dead body. She sat down instead.

"You know where the morgue is. Jane Doe 250 is in drawer nine." Doctor Dru waved her hand in that direction. Lilah turned, and walked to the door that adjoined the office and the morgue.

Lilah winced ad she opened the door. Death never smelled good, even in the clean, sanitized morgue. Jane Doe, though cleaned and prepared, was still going to have the rotten tang of fish left out in the sun. But, there might be something else. And she was going to find out.

Opening drawer nine, she realized she was right. The smell was outrageous. Being half-vampire gave her a heighted sense of smell, far superior to a normal human. Steeling herself, Lilah bent over the corpse and took a sniff. And then another. There were conflicting odors. The ocean was definitely present, but there was something non-fishy, something mammalian. There was something else, not living, and quite possibly medicinal. But the other smell, Lilah knew it. She's smelled it once or twice in centuries past. It was wolf. Not just any wolf, but homo-lupin... werewolf. The woman had been killed with a werewolf to the face.

Lilah didn't know Seattle had any lycanthropes, let alone wolves. Werewolves were almost never solitary, running and living in packs. From what she remembered, they tended to shy away from big cities, in order to keep from harming the humans and showing the world that they exist. The biggest, non-spoken rule in the supernatural comminutes was: don't get caught. If the human world knew about werewolves, they'd be hunted to extinction. Or there would be war, like with the vampires, or even the fae. So a werewolf kill? That was bad news, and Lilah knew she couldn't explain it to Doctor Collins.

Lilah took one more sniff, that other smell, the chemical one. It had a familiar tang to it. For the life of her she couldn't place it. It was going to drive her nuts, but she needed to focus on what she knew for now. Lilah needed to talk to Dru, and then she needed to take a trip to the nightclub *Ravens*. She had met the owner, Liam Campbell on another case. He knew about Vampires, had some in his club. So it wasn't a stretch to think he'd know about lycanthropes as well. Lilah covered the body back up, noticing the slight ink marks on her right hand, and hoped a finger print match came back soon. She shut the door to number nine, and went back to the Medical Examiner.

"Well?" Dru seemed impatient, but Lilah knew it was out of care for her "patients" verses a problem with Lilah herself. Lilah shook her head. She couldn't tell her it was a lycanthrope. But she had to tell the doctor something.

"You're right. There is no metal there. Our Jane Doe wasn't shot. It was likely some kind of wild animal." It was correct, to a point. Before Doctor Dru could answer, Lilah changed the subject: "Did you get answer back on her fingerprints?"

"Not yet, it's going through the database. You can bet I'll call you as soon as I know. This girl, I don't know her story, but whatever was done to her," she shook her head, "No one deserves that. She also had old bruises on her arms, and stomach. Someone had been hitting her. Her death may have been quick, but her life was brutal. I expect you to fix this." Doctor Dru wagged a finger at the Lieutenant.

"You know I will." Lilah nodded her good-bye to the doctor, and left the office.

Chapter Six

As Lilah left the hospital, the velvet violet of night was starting to settle in. The sun was down and she could move freely from the hospital to *Ravens* without hindrance. Night time was the best time. The people, the smell of the night, and all of the colors all around her. There was nothing she liked better, while working homicide and when she was on her own. To her, all life began at night. The sounds were louder, the night was bolder, people were deeper, and more magical. It wasn't just the supernatural that came out at night; it was also those humans with "gifts", the "sight" and even those who just got "hunches" and "feelings". Lilah stayed away from them the best she could, but knew it was night that drew these people out with her. It was those who were up with the sun that would never understand the true richness of any city, any town after the sun went down. And that was fine with Lilah. She liked the nights like this.

Even as she avoided the humans with magic, she couldn't help but feel the night itself wind its way around every living and dead thing. Pull at her and tempt her to grab it with her hands, and play with it like clay. Molding it to her whims, and open her up to power she refused to even dream of. If she let herself be drawn into the magic of the night, she might do two things: raise a red flag to her presence here, or lose the rest of her soul. Lilah would not risk her soul for all the power in the United States. She needed her humanity, and she held it close like a warm coat on cold winter nights.

Lilah didn't know for sure what would happen, but it wasn't worth the risk. She liked who she had become, a Lieutenant in the Seattle PD who helped people and solved murders.

Lilah walked closer to the nightclub, and could hear loud music from nearly a block away. It hadn't been that loud the last night she was there, but perhaps this was a special night. Lilah smiled to herself as the sign came into view: the background color was red, too bright to be blood, too dark to mean anything else and in black, two ravens circled each other, as though they'd dropped through the air, though never touching, facing each other for all eternity. There was a line, which didn't surprise her. It was a popular night spot, and gave the pretense of being the new fashionable place to frequent in Seattle. Next to the line stood a mountain of a man whom Lilah surmised must be the new bouncer, the old one having confessed to a murder he didn't commit, and now serving a life sentence up in Walla Walla. Lilah pulled her badge from her coat, and walked up to him.

"Get in line." He had a higher voice than she expected, and slightly clipped. A hint of an accent, most likely Ukrainian.

"I don't believe I need to." Lilah showed him her badge, and added "If you're worried about it, tell Campbell that Lilah is here to see him." She fell into the habit of using last names like she did at work. The bouncer looked at her disdainfully, but opened the door and spoke to someone just behind it in hushed tones. Shutting it again, he looked her.

"Unless you have a warrant, I'm waiting for Mr. Campbell's okay."

Lilah shrugged. She was pretty sure Mr. Campbell would see her. It was less than five minutes when the door opened again. After another quick, hushed conversation, the bouncer turned back to her and opened the rope. Lilah gave him her most dazzling smile, and went through the door politely. It was good he let her in though; she didn't want the club losing another bouncer.

A very small, but beautiful woman ushered her quickly toward Liam's office. Once there, she gave Lilah an icy smile, and her deep green eyes were cold as she sized Lilah up.

"Can I get you anything? Something to drink perhaps? Dark red wine?"

Lilah knew she was being bated, that the woman knew her secret.

"I don't drink...wine." Lilah smiled back sweetly, and added "I'm on duty." This was true, her shift had already started. Of course, this wasn't a lead she could call in.

"If you say so. Liam will be with you shortly. Don't touch anything." The smaller woman left, her voice holding no warmth. Lilah wasn't sure what she'd done to her, but it must have been bad. Or maybe, the woman just didn't like cops.

Shaking her head, Lilah sat in one of the dark leather, stiff backed chairs Liam kept in his office. She assumed it was so he was approachable, but not bother-able. They were not exactly comfortable. While waiting, she contemplated the woman who'd brought her into the office. Lilah assumed the women was trying to intimidate her. She failed miserably.

It was only a few minutes before the door opened and Liam Campbell walked in. Lilah sighed inwardly. Liam Campbell was definitely pleasant to look at. He was all tall, pale skin, and long blond hair pulled back with a leather tie wrapped in an Armani suit. But that wasn't the most beautiful thing about him, though he was truly a beautiful man. His eyes were the color of gold, glinting in sunlight. Liam Campbell had enthralled her once with those very eyes, but had promised never to do it again. She hoped he'd keep his word, because it was so hard to look away.

"Well, Lieutenant Lilah Evans. To what do I owe the pleasure tonight? Is this on actual police business or is it personal this time." When they'd met before, he mentioned a few times that they'd have to talk, and swap stories. Lilah had no plans to open up to him however. It kept them both safe.

"Nice to see you again, Mr. Campbell. Did I somehow offend the woman who showed me in? I'm sure I'd never met her before."

"Liam, please. I know we got past that, Lilah. The answer to your question is: no and yes. My assistant manager is Katy Branter. My last bouncer's sister."

"That was in no way my fault." Lilah was immediately defensive, because she felt so sorry that Erik Branter has confessed to a crime he didn't commit, but there was no way for Lilah to save him. After all, he'd been compelled by a powerful vampire.

"She knows that. It doesn't mean she can forgive your part in, even if you had no choice. She's been a great assistant manager though, and perhaps she'll get over it.

"As for us, I'm glad you're here, Lilah." He said her name in almost a purr. Liam's voice was the kind of voice that slipped through a room, warming every each of it, and making people want to laugh, and smile. It held weight, and Lilah knew there was magic behind it. Part of her didn't give a damn though, as it made her feel so good. Like there was a light inside of her darkness.

"What brings you to *Ravens* this fine evening?"

"I'm here both as a police officer, and not. I have need of your expertise. Knowing we are both something other than human, I was hoping you'd have the information I need."

"Oh, what am I?" Liam sounded intrigued.

"A nightclub owner. That often caters to the other-than-human. Other, like me."

"Yes, I guess I am that."

Lilah could see the human on his face, but it wasn't time for stories. "I know I've been in town for a while, but I seemed to miss part of the population. What do you know about lycanthropes here in Seattle?"

Liam sat forward in his chair, all air of teasing gone from him. He looked at Lilah intently. "Why?"

"We've had a murder. And it was accomplished via werewolf."

"How do you know that?" He sounded slightly alarmed.

"I could smell it. Please Liam, I need to know where to look. The victim had been beaten regularly, and then likely had her face mauled off, killing her. She was then dumped into the Puget Sound, like she was nothing. That's information I can't tell another police officer. But I think you can help me, and right now, I need it." Lilah met his eyes. This was important. No more games.

"Damnit, Lieutenant." Liam sighed, not angry at her, but upset in general, "It sucks that you intrigue me so much. To nearly anyone else, I'd smile and politely and say I had no idea what they were talking about. Suggest they were mistaken, and send them on their way." He stood up and started to pace.

"But?"

"For one thing, I like you. If you're right, I have the information that you need to know. Information I'd never give away for free. But I'll tell you, because of who you are. And I don't mean a cop." There was no pretense. Lilah didn't have to say anything about herself. He knew, at least the important bits.

"Lycanthropes, or in this case, werewolves specifically, have a pack hierarchy. Don't take the legends seriously. Though they have to change on a full moon, they have controlled change the rest of the time."

"Wait, they *can* change anytime? Not just a full moon." To say Lilah was surprised, was an understatement.

"Not every type of lycanthrope," Lilah wanted to interrupt, but Liam shook his head and kept talking.

"But the werewolves are some of the best at it. The pack in Seattle call themselves The Beasts, and frequent a dive bar on the waterfront called *Bebe's*."

Lilah blinked. That didn't sound like a bar.

"Really, *Bebe's*?"

"Would I lie?" Lilah chose not to answer that. "It was named after that song by Heart, 'BeBe LaStrange'. Maybe it wasn't always a dive bar. It isn't really now either. But if a regular human goes in? It seems like a bunch of bikers, in leathers, and a sour faced bartender. Tends to discourage human/lycanthrope mixing. Not a friendly bunch to outsiders."

74

"Not even to your customers?"

"Not the ones that aren't them, no. It is the highest taboo to let the humans find they exist. The rumor, and I meant, I have no proof, is that if a human does find out, they disappear completely. But nothing like the dead body you found. I hear that The Beasts are usually very careful about who they know, talk to and who sees them change. But, as with everything, things happen."

"Are you saying this was a pack sanctioned hit?"

"I'm definitely not saying that. There are many reasons this could have happened. She could have seen not just a wolf, but the wrong wolf. Someone jumpy about getting caught or someone with an anger issue? I don't know Lilah. I know the packs exist, I know the rules. I don't socialize with them on a regular basis. And I can't tell how, or who caused this. I can merely give you a place to start.

"And now I'm going to ask you seriously: Please don't. Don't start, don't go there, let this one go Lilah. If they are anything like their reputation, you could get seriously hurt. Or dead."

Lilah could see the concern in his eyes. Maybe he didn't know everything about her. It was very possible a werewolf was stronger than she was. Even so, she shook her head.

"I can't, Liam. I'm a Homicide Detective. It's part of who I am and I cannot let this go. No matter what this woman saw, or did, no one deserves to die like that. Thank you, for telling me about the pack in the area. I should have known, but you're right, a very low profile has been kept." She stood.

"Since I didn't know about them?" Lilah smiled at him then. "They won't know I'm coming."

Chapter Seven

Dick Schaffer, one of the architect owners of *Schaffer, Carson and Retan Designs,* couldn't believe how great the year they were having. Money was a driving factor in his life, and his life was good. Well, it had been good. The party he'd just come from was great, then bizarre. Terrifying came last, and he hurried to his high rise apartment, *The Palisades Overlook* in downtown Seattle, which really only overlooked downtown Seattle. He scurried into the building, pasted Dave, the night door man, and looking over his shoulder as he nearly ran to the elevator. After hitting the button for the fourteenth floor, and the doors shut, he relaxed slightly. After all, it was a locked, manned building. He'd be safe now, especially once he was in his apartment. He knew he was paranoid, but that didn't mean he wasn't being followed. Better safe than dead.

While at the party someone handed him a pill, which seemed to shimmer in all the colors of a rainbow. Proving he was a party guy just like the rest of them (rather than the hard-ass they usually took him for), he swallowed the pill, washing it down with the Champaign provided by the company for the party. Smiling at his co-workers and subordinates, he sat, waited, and worried just a little about what he'd just put in his mouth.

Night Hues

At first he felt nothing. He thought maybe it was a prank, or something. After about a half an hour, he noticed his eyesight wasn't as good as usual, and he was seeing colors he knew weren't there. His mother had told him about dropping LSD in college, and he wondered if it was like this. The colors didn't matter, as he was soon filled with a new bliss. His mind opened, and the world spilled in. Colors, smells, even sounds he had never heard before. Small winged creatures flew around his head, and he was enthralled with watching them.

"They're not real," he thought, "but they are beautiful." Dick had no idea how long he sat, watching the small creatures zip back and forth. Someone, Dick wasn't sure who, passed in front of him, partying with everyone else. At first Dick though nothing of it, after all, it was just some guy. But he took a second glance as the person walked by, and stifled a gasp. It was like seeing double, except both images were different. One, was a man he didn't recognize, the other was a much taller: furry, with claws and longer teeth that he could see. The worker turned, and Dick didn't recognize him, but it was quickly evident that the guy could see him. That he could see that Dick could see what he really was. He wasn't sure if it was the drug or reality as he swore he heard a growl.

Making his excuses, Dick left, just as the paranoia started to set in; he was sure he was being followed. He shook his head, wanting the drug to wear off. He was still seeing colors, feeling the night air as though it had a weight of its own, and visions of creatures that couldn't really exist. It was amazing and frightening, and he never wanted to take that drug again.

Once safe in his apartment, he leaned against his heavily locked door, and took a breath. Everything in his apartment seemed normal, say for some strange swirling colors. Sighing, he walked to the rather lavish kitchen for an apartment, one he designed himself, of course, and started the coffee maker. Maybe the caffeine would push some of the effects away.

Suddenly there was a howl outside of his door. He knew that was ridiculous because he was on the fourteenth floor, and there couldn't be wolves there. Suddenly, the sound of nails on a chalk board, only amplified, assaulted Dick's ears. It was his door. He could see it bending inwards, toward him. Pulling out his cell phone with a shaky hand, he dialed 911.

"911, what is your emergency?"

"Someone, something is breaking into my apartment. And I'm home." Dick sounded very frightened, and the operator didn't asking about the "something".

"Yes sir, what is your address. We'll send someone immediately." Dick gave his address as quickly as he could. Just as the operator was about to say something else, the metal door flew off its hinges, and into Dick's living room. He dropped his phone and quickly squatted behind the island in his kitchen, and though an atheist, began to pray anyway.

"Our father, who art in Heaven, Howard be thy name," he whispered, having no clue what he was saying. Just as a large, black muzzle appeared around the corner of where he was, followed by yellow eyes filled with rage. In front of him, the double vision started again. He saw the wolf and the person under the fur.

"Don't hurt me, please, " He begged, taking a closer look, "I'll never tell" he blubbered, crying as he saw a huge, clawed paw swipe towards him, "you..." Dick never finished his sentence, as the werewolf swiped his chest. Dick gurgled blood; it splashed across his face, and over his kitchen. The gurgling stopped quickly when the wolf reached down, and pulled out Dick's heart. Vacant eyes starred at the creature, who gave another howl, and left the building.

"Sir, sir? The police are on their way...sir?"

Chapter Eight

Lilah left *Ravens* and headed back toward the station when her phone beeped.

"Evans."

"Report to 1525 9th Ave, apartment 1403, possible homicide. Officers on scene."

"Call Detective Davies and have him meet met there, I'm not that far out. I can be there in five minutes."

"Copy." Lilah hung up before the word was finished. She changed directions and headed for the scene. She knew it was in one the new expensive high rise apartment buildings. Lilah knew all too well that death didn't judge on socioeconomic status. She sped her walk up, cutting what should have been nearly an hour down to those five minutes she promised.

Outside the ostentatious building, *The Palisades Overlook*, stood a doorman, who was obviously on duty. Lilah slowed her walk, and went to the door.

"I'm sorry ma'am, no one is allowed in."

"I am." She badged him.

"I'm sorry Lieutenant, but we have to be careful. The scene inside is secured by two of your people. I was here all night, the only person I saw come or go was Mr. Schaffer. We aren't even close to full capacity yet, so the nighttime is slow."

"How did Mr. Schaffer seem when he came home?" Lilah turned her recorder on. "Do you mind if I record this?"

"Not at all. Was on the job in Chicago before I came out here."

"What made you quit?"

"Honestly, this pays better. Had four mouths to feed."

"Gotcha," Lilah went back to the subject at hand, "How did Mr. Schaffer seem when he came home this evening?"

"Not good. His face was pale, and his eyes were slightly...odd. And he was watching over his shoulder for something. He was scared."

"His eyes were odd? How?"

"I can't explain it fully, and he was only out here briefly. And it was dark, but they really seemed off." Seemed off? That'd be useful in her report. She clicked off the recorder.

"Thanks. When my partner, Detective Davies shows, please send him right up."

"You got it, Lieutenant."

Lilah walked into the glass and metal monstrosity and for a moment missed the old days, when a castle was the most ostentatious thing for miles. There were days she felt

82

technology was wasted. On the other hand, she was a murder cop, so what did she know?

The elevator was glass on three sides, and gave her an amazing view of the night. It was a strangely clear one, and the higher the elevator went, the more she could admire. That was her world down there. That was the nightlife in Seattle.

Stepping off the elevator the smell of fresh blood was overwhelming. Whatever she'd been called in for, it was a homicide. There were two uniformed officers by the door. One was standing, her back to the door. The other was bent over a trashcan, a bit blue, and likely a lot green. Lilah stepped up to the other office.

"He going to be okay?" Lilah pointed at the officer on the floor.

His partner, an older, graying woman whose name seemed to be Greenly, smiled a little.

"He'll be fine, sir, just a rookie. First homicide. If he's got the salt for this job, he'll get over that, sir." Her smile dimmed, "But this is a hell of a first homicide."

"Report, Greenly."

"We followed up on a 911 call that ended abruptly. The operator thought she heard a fight in the background. When we got here, the door was gone, off the hinges, and now in the living room. We took a quick look inside, saw that the resident was dead, and called it in. Sir, it's one of the worst I've ever seen, and I've been on the job twenty years." Lilah studied her face for a moment, and then nodded. She could see Greenly had been around this block a few times, and decided to cut the rookie with her some slack.

"My partner should be here soon. Don't let anyone pass except for Detective Davies. Then see if you can find your partner some water."

"Sir, one thing in St. John's defense? He didn't throw up on your crime scene." Lilah smiled.

"Good, then I don't have to kick his ass." Greenly smiled at her again. Lilah gave her a small one back, and entered the apartment. The blood mixed with visceral gore, and she could already see it splattering walls, with a slight trail of droplets leaving the kitchen. They were small, except in one spot. Someone obviously shook from themselves the droplets leading from the kitchen. There was a larger splatter pattern on the wall. The worst of it was definitely in the kitchen. The man who'd been Richard "Dick" Schaffer was on his back, staring blankly at the celling. Blood caked the walls, and the cabinets in the center island. This was a brutal and possibly personal attack.

"What a waste." Lilah murmured as she took the black nitrile gloves from her pocket. Snapping them on, she bent to look at the body. Correction, to look at Dick Shaffer. His name would keep him real to her, and drive her to solve this homicide. Unless they were unidentifiable, Lilah used their names. No one had the right to take that from them.

The gaping maw in his chest was likely the cause of death, since the arterial blood was still pumping when his heart was pulled from there. The spray around the body was dark, and thick. Doing a quick check over the rest of the body, the only other injury she saw was a slash to his neck. Not deep enough to cause him to bleed out. Otherwise, he seemed fine... Except his eyes. She took another look at his blood stained face, and the eyes clouding over with death, and noticed one small thing. They weren't the same color: brilliant royal purple for the right one, and Easter bunny yellow for the other. On a hunch, she sniffed the victim. Behind her, came the heavy footsteps of Detective Allen Davies, her partner. She'd know those boots anywhere.

"What'd you find, oh Lieutenant on high?" Always with the snark, this one. One of the many things Lilah had grown to appreciate about him.

"Thirty days for insubordination, just for you. Or perhaps a swift kick in the ass." The back and forth was normal between them. Homicide is stressful, and a bit of levity wasn't dishonoring the dead. Instead, it made them better investigators. Stress leads to mistakes, humor helped them relax, and find the answers. As she straighten up, and turned slightly away from Dick's body, she realized two things. She smelled wolf, and that strange chemical she'd now run into two other times. Perhaps it was a designer drug she wasn't aware of yet? She made a mental note to contact the specific drug unit, in Vice.

"Okay, this may be one of the grossest things I've seen." Her partner gagged just once, holding the rest down. Lilah could count on Davies to do his job.

"I've taken a look. Your thoughts?"

"If I didn't know better, I'd say animal attack, and a large one. Lion or tiger maybe. But there are no lions or tigers lose on the fourteenth floor of this building, and neither could blow the door out like that. Perhaps a drug addict using something like Angel Dust? I know we haven't seen a lot of it lately, but maybe it's catching back on?" Davies was guessing, Lilah knew. She'd have made the same guess, if she couldn't smell what was under all that blood.

"Do me a favor, and look at his eyes for me." Davies crouched by the body, and ignoring the huge hole for now, he studied the eyes, as Lilah asked.

"Uh, Lieutenant, his eyes look like he's part of the egg hunt in Pioneer Square every Easter. They're fading fast behind death, but neither of those colors occurs naturally."

"Exactly. There is the possibly that he's odd, and is wearing contacts. It is after work hours. We'll talk to Doctor Dru about that. But it is an anomaly. Okay, now the rest of your observations." Lilah looked him in the face as Davies stood back up, looking a bit green. For a seasoned Detective, this body hit him hard. To be fair, this was a horrific death. Maybe everyone reacted like that to the brutality that shortened Dick's life. For Lilah, it was the loss of another human life that bothered her. Death never did.

"This wasn't a robbery; nothing seems out of place or removed, except his heart. This was a targeted attack. Maybe the heart is significant. Like a spouse or other spurned lover?"

"Not a bad speculation. Head back to the station and follow that up? I have another line to tug. If it pans out, I'll let you know." Well, what she could tell him, anyway.

"Call me when you have a handle on the life of Dick Shaffer. I should be in later, and we can go over it. This is going to end up more high profile than the lady of the other day. So we'll have the media to deal with as well. Not one word to the press until the captain orders us to speak to them."

"Yeah, like I didn't know that," Davies huffed, "I'll see you at the station Lieutenant."

Chapter Nine

Leaving the high-rise apartments, Lilah started toward the hospital and then changed her mind. Dru Collins didn't even have the body yet, so there'd be no answers to be had there. Instead, she headed for the 9th precinct and the Vice crew. If there was a new drug on the streets, they were usually the first to know.

Walking in the doors, Lilah went straight to the bullpen. Her favorite night-time Vice officer was sitting at his desk.

"Damien Hunter!" He lifted his head from his work, and smiled.

"Lilah Evans. The only weirder cop than me." He laughed, and Lilah joined in. They both loved the night shift and they both loved those freakier cases. They'd even shared a drink or two, but that was a while back.

"Good to see you! I've got a weird one for you, though you might have a line on a new synthetic drug." Hunter gave her hard eyes for a moment and then softened.

"This is about a homicide isn't it?"

"At least two. I'm not trying to take your place, you know that. I love Homicide. But I think we may have overlap. I'm not completely sure what it does, but it messes with the takers eyes." Lilah stopped, watching Hunter's face. He knew something.

"Damn it. I'd hoped it was isolated, just another version of a hallucinogenic we were aware of. But the few guys we've pulled in on the stuff? They're not acting in a way consistent with other hallucinogens. The closest to normal, is their claim that they can see the truth in the dark. Not quite sure what they means. But it's their eyes, Evans, you're right. They turn colors of no eyes I've even seen. And sometimes quite rapidly." Hunter sighed.

"And there's been one fatality. So far. Street name: Rainbow. We haven't been able to get our hands on any to analyze." He looked at Lilah again, "Quid pro quo?"

"I have a man in lock-up who may have killed someone. He was standing over a body, and not exactly coherent about it. I have another in the morgue. Attacked by something or someone big in his apartment, I should say, his locked apartment. Heart ripped out. But he died quickly enough, that his eyes stayed an unnatural shade of royal purple in one, and Easter egg yellow, at least long enough for me and Davies to see it. I'm hoping for contacts, but…"

"…they probably aren't." Hunter finished for her.

Lilah nodded. That was definitely one of her fears with this new drug.

"Evans, we have one in lock-up right now. Do you want to talk with her? After all, the drug seems to be in conjunction with your cases."

"Of course, you'll want reciprocation." Lilah noted dryly.

"You wound! Of course, you're correct, but still, you wound."

"And you're an idiot." What should have been an insult was full of laughter. "Lead on, MacDuff."

The holding cells were on the third floor of the smaller precinct. It was an odd set up, with some administrative offices on the second floor. Lilah missed the smells and sights of the main SPD. Vice always smelled too clean. Hunter ushered her into integration one, where a wall of body odor and piss smacked hard into her already sensitive nose. Under that, lurked the strange smell of Rainbow. Behind the table sat a young blond girl, of no more than nineteen. Lilah supposed she would have been beautiful cleaned up, but the filth that caked her skin, and nearly fell from her hair hid the kid behind it.

"Lieutenant Lilah Evans, this is Gracie Roman. In for public intoxication, assault and resisting arrest. We haven't gotten a lot coherent out of her. Feel free to see if you can." He gave Lilah a smile, and left the room. She knew he'd be watching through the one-way glass.

Lilah sat across from Gracie, who'd had her eyes closed since her arrest. Lilah touched her hand lightly, and the girl stirred.

"Gracie, my name is Lilah. Will you look at me please?"

"Lady, I don't need to look to see. It's all around us. Even behind my lids I can see the colors. Dancing and singing." That was the kind of drugged out answer Lilah expected.

"First, it's not Lady, its Lieutenant. Second, open your eyes and look at me." The force in Lilah's voice had Gracie open her eyes quickly and she gave out a quick but urgent scream and closed them again.

"I don't want to look at you lad...I mean Lieutenant. What is wrong with your face?" Good question, Lilah had no idea what Gracie saw. Lilah did get a look at Gracie's eyes however, and they were changing from one impossible color to the next.

"What do you think you saw?" Luckily, Lilah knew it would come across as drug ramblings to Hunter.

"Where are your eyes? Oh my god, where are your eyes? And fangs, you have fangs. You're a demon from hell!!!" Gracie shrieked again, clawing at her face. Hunter came rushing in as Lilah stood to try and stop the girl from hurting herself.

"Hunter, this girl needs medical attention NOW."

"No shit!" Hunter grabbed her hands, while Lilah called 911.

"We need an ambulance at the 9th police precinct. Possible drug overdose, we fear the prisoner is doing herself harm. Synthetic drug, street name Rainbow. Yes, thank you." Lilah hung up. "They're on their way. What can I do?"

"Wait for the aide car outside. I can't have you in here right now. I have no idea what she saw when she looked at you, but I know it wasn't good. I'm sorry, Lilah."

"You're not wrong. I'll let them in." Hunter certainly had a point. This didn't look or sound good. Lilah never had fangs, only slightly sharper than normal canines. What the hell did Rainbow really do?

She left interrogation quickly, and took the stairs in seconds. As she waited for the aide car, Lilah had some idea now of what the drug did, though she'd need another test subject or two. Her fear was that it allowed the mundane to see the supernatural: which was a great reason for murder.

After the ambulance arrived and bundled Gracie Roman off to the psychiatric ward at Seattle General, she started to head out.

"Lieutenant, wait…"

"What's up?" The sun was peeking over the horizon, and it had been a long night. Still, she couldn't excuse herself for that.

"What the hell happened in there? I was watching, but I'm telling you, all I saw, you were talking to her, and she started clawing her eyes out. What the hell did you say? I couldn't quite make it out."

"All I did was tell her to look at me. I thought I was plenty loud about it, because she opened her eyes. But she didn't see me, Lieutenant Lilah Evans. Instead, she saw me as some kind of monster. Old monster movie type."

"A monster?" Hunter's voice was incredulous. "And you weren't even interrogating her at your most bitchy." He'd obviously calmed down some, if he could make a joke like that. Lilah decided not to even call him on it.

"I wonder how common it is, that this drug causes monster visions? I can see that leading to violence." Hunter mused.

"You're not wrong. After you talk to a few more, would you let me know?" Lilah knew the answer, but how could she share it? This was a nightmare for everyone involved. "Let me know what happens to poor Gracie."

"Yeah, I'll call. Take care of yourself. And don't forget that quid pro quo."

"Of course not Hunter. Have a good one." Lilah gave him a quick smile, and headed out into the quickly fading blues and now pinks of the night. She was certain there wouldn't be much sharing of information on her part.

Chapter Ten

Lilah's phone rang just as she slipped inside the Derringer building. It was the closest and had an old access tunnel that lead toward the Underground.

"Evans."

"I heard you had an adventure at Vice without me."

"That's because you're the sidekick and I'm the superhero." Lilah was snarky at her partner. Luckily, she could count on him to be snarky back.

"Yeah, a lame one, like Aquaman."

"Hey, he's not lame. He controls all the armies of Atlantis!"

"If you say so: nerd."

"Was there something you wanted Davies, or just felt you needed to get on my nerves before bed time?"

"Can't I do both, sir?"

"Every day. Now what's up?" Banter time over.

"I finished at Schaffer's. It was one hell of a mess. The first on scene found one person who claimed to have heard a dog howl, but that's it. The body should be at the morgue by now. There was some hair left on scene, it's with the lab guys. And after you tell me about Rainbow and I file my report I'm heading home as well."

"A dog huh?" Lilah knew better, "and where did you hear about Rainbow?"

"A girl was transported from vice at 0430 this morning, having a very bad trip. It's hard hide after that." He wasn't wrong, Lilah knew.

"It's whatever is causing the victims eyes to change. A new, synthetic hallucinogen. It's been known to lead to violent outbursts, and even in a few cases death. Schaffer had definitely been taking it, though we'll double check his blood work. It's some bad shit, Davies. The girl in vice started to claw her eyes out, due to whatever she was seeing."

"Shit Evans, I'm not sure I wanted to hear that."

"And I wasn't thrilled seeing it, but it's a new reality for us. Get some sleep. We have some rough days coming. Go home. Do your report tonight."

"Yes sir!" Davies hung up, and Lilah finished her trek back to her little apartment before the burgeoning coral sky turned any lighter.

Lilah made it to her apartment, and nearly fell into bed. This case had a lot of bad vibes and even perhaps magic around it. It drained her, make her feel insignificant. Lilah knew if she'd just embrace her magic she'd have this solved in a day, or in a moment. But that was a dangerous slope and she knew it. Well, she thought it, and that was good enough.

Sighing, she closed her eyes, hoping to get in a few solid hours of shut-eye.

Buzz. Buzz.

"Shit," she sat up fully, pulling her phone from her back pocket.

"This better be important." Lilah growled into her phone.

"Did I wake you up?" Doctor Dru, who sounded perfectly put together over the phone at 6am.

"As a matter of fact... What's up doc?" Dru didn't laugh. It must be something serious.

"The first victim, pulled out of Puget Sound? We've got an ID. Please get down here now."

"You can't tell me on the phone." Lilah heard her bed calling to her.

"No. Find a way, just get here." The good doctor hung up the phone, without another word. She was shaken by something.

Lilah toyed with the idea of waking up Davies, but decided against it. He deserved a bit of rest, and if Lilah needed her extra abilities, she wasn't ready to explain it to Davies. It's coming someday, just not yet.

She changed her clothes, adjusted her should holster so it fit neatly under her jacket and headed off. Lilah knew underground usually took ten minutes, but shaved off a few, just by hurrying a bit more than usual. She arrived in the usual way, via the sub-basement, and got onto the bottom floor with no one seeing her. Luckily, this was Dr. Drusilla Collins haunt, so to speak. Both her office and the city/SPD morgue were down here.

Lilah made her way swiftly to Dr. Dru's office. Dru stood there, staring into the morgue. It seemed odd somehow.

"Hey Doc, I'm here." The doctor rounded on Lilah, her face a mixture of agony, fear and anger.

"What the hell happened here Lieutenant? I have two bodies that look as though an animal came through and ate them. And there's a girl upstairs who tore her eyes out after looking at you. Just what in the hell is going on?"

"Damn. Last I saw Gracie, she'd just tried to claw at her eyes. She clawed them completely out?" Lilah felt a little sick.

"The E.M.T.'s couldn't get her restrained fast enough. Once she was out of the station, she literally stuck her fingers in her eyes, and pushed. What the hell, Lilah?"

Lilah shook her head. No matter what she told the doctor, this could only end badly.

"Doctor Collins, there are two things I can do here. I can give you the company line with a little strange insight like I always do. Or, I can tell you the absolute truth. But once I do that, there's no going back, and no promise of safety."

The doctor sat down in her chair, and furrowed brow. She could tell that Lilah was serious. Dru pursed her lips, and nodded. It was time to know what was really going on in Seattle.

"All of it, Lilah. Then we'll go look at the bodies with new eyes."

Before Lilah started talking, she checked the hallway outside of the office door. Empty. She then shut and locked the doctor's office door, and made sure any other way in or out was shut.

"On the streets right now, is a new synthetic hallucinogen. It starts out normal, as far as we can tell, except for the eyes. The strange colors that they change are a side effect. It creates violent outbursts," Lilah took a deep breath, "and they start seeing things that are real, but hidden from the human world." Lilah tried to rush through that last sentence.

"Wait. What do you mean 'real but hidden'?"

"This is the part you didn't want to know."

"I told you, I want all of it. Every last bit."

"You must keep everything I tell you to yourself. I mean it, this can't go past that door."

"Who am I going to tell? Them?" Dru waved her hand vaguely at the morgue. "I work so much, these are my best friends."

"Promise me, please."

"Fine. I promise. Now spill."

It was close enough, Lilah knew. Drusilla dripped with integrity, and her word was iron clad. The good doctor wasn't going to tell anyone.

"The things that go bump in the night that you tell yourself can't exist. It's the wind. Or a tree. Chills when it's warm out, or someone walked over your grave, and other lies humans tell each other in the dark or when they are scared." Dru looked like she wanted to interrupt, but instead let Lilah keep going.

"The night hides most of us. For most of the nightlife, they prefer to stay away from humans. It's our first rule. As long as we keep to the night, we don't get hunted to extinction. It wasn't until recently that I learned Seattle had more than just me lurking in the dark. There were rumors of course, but again, the point was to hide, even from each other.

"There are vampires. Werewolves. Fae, or I'm pretty sure there are fae, they're tricky on purpose. These, are the only ones I've had run-ins with, and most of that was here in Seattle, which took over two-hundred years. Before that, I thought it was just us. There could be much more out in Washington's night. Or other places in the world."

Questions ran across the doctor's face. But she took in the knowledge, and sat thoughtfully for a moment.

"And what are you?" Drusilla had known for a long time that Lilah was something more, different, but she hadn't wanted to know before.

"I'm known as *homo-sapiens sanguineous.* Verses my father, who is just *homo-sanguineous.*"

"So, if I'm following the nomenclature correctly, your father was, or is a full vampire. And you are half-vampire. What does that mean? " Doctor Dru put her head in her hands.

"It means I still hold part of my human soul. I was born with some humanity, and empathy. And I have some of the, for lack of a better word, powers of the vampire. As well as some of their weaknesses."

"I don't know if I should believe you, or admit you in psych consult."

"Want a small piece of proof, that I am at the very least, not normal?"

"What, want to bite me?" It was supposed to be a joke, but came out bitter and harsh.

"I don't bite. I don't drink human blood. She paused; this was a lot harder than expected. "Do you have a mirror?" Dru opened her desk drawer and pulled out a compact. She handed it to Lilah wordlessly.

Lilah opened it, and then walked to Dru so they could both be seen in the mirror.

"What color are my eyes, doctor?"

"I don't know. It never occurred to me to look. Usually I notice things like that. Isn't that odd?"

"It never occurs to anyone, look in the mirror, you'll see why."

Dru looked up, shook her head as if she didn't believe it, and then looked again, closer.

"You have no eyes. It's grey, misty...how can that be?"

"Never fear, I have eyes. After all, I can see you. For the most part, people just don't look. Vampirism is a parasite. It eats the human soul. That's why most vampires, or so my father said, can't be seen in mirrors, nor can they see themselves. I can see everything except my eyes. Being what I am, half of that darkness, I carry the parasite within me. So my eyes don't show up in mirrors. But it's just my eyes."

Dru shook her head. "So much information, and yet, I know there is more. This is one moment in my awakening to the supernatural. And it's a big one. So there are vampires. What else?"

"The two bodies that came in? The ones you could swear were mauled, though it doesn't quite add up? After all, this is the big city, and the only animals that could even come close to that kind of damage are restricted to Woodland Park Zoo. Which would be true, if you were looking for nothing but an animal. Sadly, I'm not the only being in Seattle that passes for human. There are werewolves. If you can accept vampires, I hope you can accept werewolves, too. And likely other things, but so far, I can only prove what I've verified for myself."

"You've seen a werewolf?" Dru sounded dubious.

"No. But I've smelled one. Both bodies, the one from the harbor and the one from the high rise, smell like wolf. And drugs. The same drug."

"The one you were mentioning earlier. That can let 'normal' people see the supernatural?"

"The very same. In house, we're calling it Rainbow."

"I've got this one," Dru sighed, "because of the odd colored eyes."

"Exactly. The girl upstairs tore out her eyes, because she could see what I really am. Didn't do much for the ego." Humor: the last vestige of the desperate. Lilah hoped

Drusilla believed her. "Is there any chance the eyes are contacts?"

"No."

The doctor just sat, staring at Lilah for a few minutes. Her eyes were hard, and angry. At what, Lilah wasn't sure.

"Doc?"

"Give me a minute. I'm wrapping my head around this, the best I can." Lilah just nodded and let Drusilla sit in peace. The passage of time stopped as Lilah waited for her to speak again.

"Okay. I'm pissed Lilah. I won't lie. I'm angry as hell that I didn't know, about the supernatural, about you. This is why you take the weird cases. Oh, and only work at night. If you'd just been honest with me, many of my autopsies for you would have turned out differently. And you know it." Dru let out a heavy breath, "At the same time, I can't blame you. But from now on, just between us, no more lies. I'm a doctor, and a scientist, I need to know what I'm looking at when someone is on my table. We'll figure out the mundane answers for everyone else together, but I need to know what I'm looking at from now on, or I can't do my damned job. Deal?"

There was no other choice.

"Deal."

Chapter Eleven

With the hard part behind them, Doctor Collins and Lilah went to take another look at the bodies in the morgue.

"You were going to tell me about the first body." Lilah prodded the doctor.

"Yes. I still am. Her name was Felice Stephens." The name meant nothing to Lilah.

As they stood over her body one more time, Lilah tried to see the woman who once lived in the now pile of flesh and bone, with no face. She couldn't picture her, no matter how hard she tried.

"Who was she?"

"That's the thing, Lilah. She was just an average woman. She had a boyfriend, a small apartment and worked part time at a bar downtown. Her bloodwork came back flagged for the new hallucinogenic." Lilah had a sick feeling.

"The bar downtown where she worked? *Bebe's* by any chance?"

"How did you know that? Don't tell me there's some power you have to read my mind" the doctor inquired with a frown.

"Nothing as exciting as that. I have a long-shot lead that involves that bar. Only I'm not sure it's so long anymore. I need to do a background check on her, and see if she has a further connection. Though working there might be enough." Lilah sighed.

"When you first saw this body, what did you notice?" Doctor Dru already heard this once, but wanted it again.

"She smelled of wolf, and something else. That something else, as you know, was Rainbow".

"And you let me believe it was something else..."

"We've now been over this. I'm sorry." Lilah shrugged.

"You're right. I'm sorry. It's just so much to take in." The doctor shook her head, as she rolled Felice's body back into the drawer, and opened the next one.

"And this man, um..." Doctor Dru checked the notes, "Dick Schaffer. What happened here?"

"Sadly, almost exactly what it looks like. Mr. Schaffer had also taken Rainbow and who knows what he saw while on it."

"Okay, Mr. Schaffer heart was removed forcefully by a werewolf." Drusilla sighed, "I can't believe I just said that aloud. That cause of death isn't going to fly for the legal documents. We're going with a knife on this one, and staying with the shot in the face for Ms. Stephens. Does that work for you Lieutenant?"

"Yes, sadly it does. I'll work out the broken door and all that from Mr. Schaffer's house. Probably a large man out of his mind on Angel Dust."

"That excuse isn't going to fly forever. Phencyclidine isn't seen as much as it was in the 1970's and 1980's. Methamphetamine is more likely these days. If we're going to do this, we should do it right." The doctor was even particular when it came to falsifying records. This was useful for Lilah, though it didn't stop her from feeling bad about it.

"Then I'll go with methamphetamine in my report. You can report the presence Rainbow in both bodies, because vice has already picked up on the drug. Of course, all they know is the weird eyes, hallucinations and possible violent outbursts."

"And the girl upstairs?"

"She saw something behind my human face. Even I don't know what that is. I'd like to think it was just my eyes. The evidence though, screams something else. Yes, it's my fault she's upstairs, and blind. I may never forgive myself, but I had no control over what she saw, or her actions."

"Lilah," the doctor said softly, "I wasn't blaming you. I was merely asking."

"That's ok. I blame myself."

Chapter Twelve

It was nearly noon, as Lilah found her way back to the basement, and the hidden passages further down. Exhausted she made her way home as quickly as she could while avoiding the sunlight. Once inside, she pulled out her phone. Tired or not, it was time to wake up Davies. He needed to know about the girl, maybe he could put in some time finding out more about Felice Stephens.

"What?" Detective Allen Davies voice was gruff. Lilah knew she must have woken him.

"There's been movement on the dead body I found in the water. Her name was Felice Stephens. And she worked at *Bebe's* bar, down off the wharf. I need to you look further into her background. Leave *Bebe's* to me, I'll go tonight." Lilah was matter-of-fact. She wasn't in the mood for a fight.

"Sir, are you sure?" Polite, weird.

"Yes. After looking into her data, I want you and Harper to take the apartment. Interview her neighbors, and tackle her apartment. I doubt there is much there, but it's worth a look. Harper needs more field experience, and you're just the guy to give it to her." Lilah swore that didn't sound dirty in her head.

"Yes boss. I guess we'll meet in the middle."

"Sounds about right. I'll fill you in then. Be safe out there." Lilah hung up. She wasn't much for goodbyes.

Lilah pulled a steak out of the fridge and ate it was it was. Too tired to be civilized and heat it up. Took three bites, and it was gone. Sitting on the bed, she removed her shoes, and leaned back into her pillows, and fell into the blessed darkness of sleep.

Seven hours later, she was up, and ready to face *Bebe's* on the waterfront. She dressed darkly, from the black jeans, and tee, to her dark leather coat. The Sig Saur under the jacket in its holster was almost invisible, unless she took her coat off. Perfect for talking to resistive, preternatural creatures like werewolves. The night was blustery, and likely cold, though she couldn't feel it. Even though it was early evening, the dark began to swirl around her, inviting her to explore it, and the possibilities it held. Sometimes, the pull of it was intoxicating. At the moment it was just irritating. Lilah had one goal, and it wasn't to play with, or avoid the lure of the night. Tonight, there were wolves in the darkness.

It really was a shack, with a faded blue and white wooden sign that merely said BEBE'S. A couple of neon signs in the window indicating they had beer. The soft orange glow proclaimed they carried "Rainer Beer". Lilah doubted that local microbrews were on the menu. The old peeling, and slightly warped wooden door opened with ease for Lilah, and she walked into the dimly lit bar. It gave off the rich smell of well-worn leather and underneath, the smell of animal, of violence, with a faint whiff of forest. It smelled of wolf. Faces turned to stare at her, many giving her the evil eye, and other creepy faces. She assumed it was to scare of any unwanted customers who weren't pack. Lilah wondered for a brief moment, if they could smell her too.

Passing the scowling and disdainful customers, she made her was up to the bar. Dark and shiny mahogany wasn't quite what she expected. The bartender wasn't either. Sizing him up before he turned to her, he was tall, well over 6'5", and nearly as dark as the bar itself. Dreadlocks with multicolored beads fell past his shoulders, which seemed wider than the space between the bar and the booze. Yet he moved with ease. When he turned to her, she felt a jolt from his deep green eyes. Eyes that weren't happy she was there.

"Get out." He growled.

"Isn't this a bar, open to the public?"

"I have the right to refuse service to anyone. This isn't your scene lady. So get out."

"I haven't asked for a drink, so you're not being asked to serve me, Mister..."

"Fenris."

"You've got to be joking."

"Do I look like I'm joking, lady?"

"I guess not. So, Mr. Fenris, I'm looking for someone to talk to about Felice Stephens." Behind her in the taproom, she felt tensions rise.

"It's just Fenris. I'm sorry, I don't know the name." He wasn't a bad liar, as those things go. Lilah just knew better.

"I find that hard to believe, as this was her place of employment. I would assume you know your staff." Fenris stiffened slightly.

"You must mean Fe. She hasn't been here in a while. I assumed she quit, she had talked about moving to Portland. What's it to you anyway?"

"Oh how rude of me," Lilah didn't feel rude at all, as she pulled her badge from her pocket. "I'm Lieutenant Lilah Evans of SPD, homicide division. I'm looking into the murder of Felice Stephens." Dishes fell to the floor somewhere in the back, behind the bar. A tall, thin man came out from a swinging door, his face pale, sweat beading on his forehead.

"Did you just say Fe was dead?" asked the nervous man.

"I did. And you are?"

"Keith Richmond. I work here, mostly bussing and doing dishes. Fe was a waitress. But, like Fenris said, I haven't seen her for weeks." Keith sat down hard on a stool. Fenris watched him coolly for a moment.

"Keith, go home."

"Not just yet, I have some questions." Lilah tried to remain matter of fact, even as Keith stood. "Sit down Mr. Richmond." Keith looked from Lilah then back to Fenris, with something closer to fear in his eyes.

"This is my bar, Lieutenant. I say Keith goes home, he goes home."

"Your bar?" Lilah raised an eyebrow in disbelief. "If I tell you that I need to talk to him, to anyone here really, and they stay here until I've talked to them. This is a murder investigation, not swing night at the VFW." Fenris looked angry and confused. Lilah aged herself a little bit with the last analogy. She decided to let it slide.

Fenris leaned over the bar quickly, sniffing her hair and neck before recoiling slightly.

"What are you?"

"Lieutenant, Homicide. I told you that."

"Maybe you are, and maybe you aren't. But you're something else. You are not human."

"Speak for yourself wolf-boy." The air tightened around Lilah, the night suddenly hot and prickly with power. Not the seductive power that she knew to be the night, but something that promised violence, and strangely, freedom. From behind her, she heard the lock click, and realized she might have let the dog out of the bag too soon.

Fenris walked around the bar, and faced her solidly. He had a good foot of height on her, and some very obvious hard won muscle. He radiated power. It was heavy, and slapped at her own abilities, almost playfully. He was powerful. However, she suspected he wasn't pack leader powerful.

"You smell of blood, and old death. Of power, and darkness. So I ask again: what are you?" He asked in a low growl.

"You smell of dog, and leather. Of the forest, of violence and blood. You have power, Fenris. But, I don't think you have enough."

The fist was fast, and hard, catching her left cheek with a loud crack and knocking her backward. Because she wasn't expecting it, she ended up on the floor.

"How is that for power?"

"You want me to critique your punch?" Lilah said, with only a slight mumble. Her cheek stung a little, but it was a blow she suspected would have dislocated a human's jaw. Or worse.

Lilah took her time getting up. Not because she had to, but because it was expected.

"Let's compare." Lilah hit the man back, aiming as always for the wall behind him as her fist connected with his face. Surprise showed in his face as he stumbled backward, and down to one knee. Lilah looked down at him.

"Are you done?" He wasn't. His fist came up fast, connecting solidly with her stomach. She felt it, but dismissed it as she rammed her knee into his solar plexus and punched him again in the face as he doubled over, sending him flying backward and into a wall. He crumpled below it for a moment, and Lilah felt and heard some of the patrons stand.

"Stay out of it," Fenris growled from the floor. "This is my fight."

"This is a stupid fight," Lilah added. "I merely was asking for information."

"I don't believe you." He'd pulled his impressive frame back up from the floor, took two steps toward her, put everything he had behind it, and smashed her face with his fist again, this time hitting the edge of her nose and right cheek. It was a more solid punch, with power behind it. Lilah fell back into the bar with enough force, that if she'd been human, ribs would have broken. Lilah didn't bruise or break like humans, but knew she'd be black and blue for a little while after this fight.

Fenris moved closer, ready to land another blow when Lilah kneed him in the balls, doubling him over again, and this time at the same time, landing a secondary kick to the side of his knee. Fenris let out a cry, as he knee crunched to the side satisfactorily.

"Stay down," Lilah growled. She didn't really want him to stay down, her primal instincts kicking in, wanting the kill. Lilah hadn't killed anyone in nearly a century. She didn't want to fall of the wagon now.

Fenris looked up at her, pain written in his eyes and face. Even so, he kept the deep bravado in his voice, "I'll fucking kill you bitch!" He tried to rise on the dislocated knee, and she readied herself to hit him again, when a voice cut in from the taproom. Lilah nearly forgot she had an audience. Some cop she was.

"Fenris, stay down. This stops now!" A deep voice came through the swinging door. Lilah kept her eyes on Fenris, but could feel power, heat walking closer. Fenris was powerful, but compared to what was coming her way, he was completely junior league. Fenris sent a dark look behind her.

"But..."

"No buts. She beat you, pure and simple. If she'd been wolf, she'd kill you and take your place in the pack. As she isn't, you should feel ashamed. She may not be pack, but she is powerful. Which if you hadn't been a fool, you'd have noticed before you threw the first punch." The man, who was shorter than Fenris, with a dark complexion and an easy smile stood in front of her, taking her gaze away from Fenris.

"Erick, Tom, please take Fenris in the back and see that he gets patched up. Make sure he turns, and heals the knee. I'm pretty sure the Lieutenant here dislocated it, and possibly broke the bone as well. Call Ingrid if you have to." With that, he dismissed Fenris.

"And you are?" Lilah asked, still in a fighting stance.

"Calm down lady. I'm not going to fight you. Let's have a seat."

"Fine with me. Could I get some ice please?" Lilah probably didn't need it, but she'd play the injured damsel while it suited her. For now, this man, whom she was assuming was the pack leader, was being reasonable. She sat back on one of the stools, and waited.

"Keith, get the lady some ice." He didn't even check to see if Keith did as he was told. This was a man who expected to be obeyed. Keith came back with one of those icepacks you have to crunch to make cold. Lilah tried to smile at him, and winced. Her face did hurt, just enough. She leaned into the cold, as she held it to her face.

"Are we civilized now?" Her voice held a level of sarcasm.

"We are usually civilized. I'm Ulric."

"Where do you get your names? Baby Wolves R Us? Fenris is Norse. Your name is an English variant." She wasn't feeling sociable, or nice. Ulric just laughed, a deep warm laughter she wanted to cuddle up in. But Lilah knew better. Some of it was power. And some of it was just a great laugh.

"Well now, Lieutenant, that is probably a discussion for another day. If we have one."

"Another day?" She readied for attack.

"No, another discussion. Which could be in our future. Time will tell. As it is right now, I want to help with your investigation. But first, how did you know we were wolves?"

Lilah sighed. "Because you smell like wolves."

"Because we smell like wolves...that simple?"

"You know it isn't. Aren't you going to ask what I am?"

"No Ma'am. I don't think so. Maybe during another conversation. I have my suspicions regardless. However, you're here about a murder. Let's talk about that."

"At this point, uh, Ulric, I'd like it to be just you, me and Keith. I don't normally discuss a murder investigation with a whole bar."

"Are you up for walking? I have an office in back. It's not much, but it's private." Ulric smiled.

"As you like. Walking will be no problem, for me." It was a dig at Fenris, who wasn't even in the room.

"Alright everyone, show is over. Go back to whatever." Ulric said, addressing the room. "Keith, come with us." Though he looked shaky still, he stood and followed the both of them into the back. As she was walking away, Lilah noticed someone slide behind the bar, and take Fenris' place.

Chapter Thirteen

The office in back was done all in shades of dark mahogany and muted chrome. One thing Lilah could say for Ulric, he kept his office clean. She expected piles of paper, perhaps a smaller room, and a beer odor. Instead, she could have been in any CEO's office for any major company. Except for a cot on the right wall. Lilah suspected that Ulric spent more time in his office than anywhere else.

Lilah took one of the two chairs on the opposite side of Ulric's desk, letting Keith take the other one. As Ulric took his seat, Lilah got a good look at Keith. He looked strung out, tired, pale, and shaking. He could be reacting to the news that Felice Stephens was dead. Or that she'd found a body he'd dumped. Lilah wasn't sure which yet.

"So Lieutenant Evans, why did you stop by? I was listening, but got sidetracked by the fight. Did you say one of my employees was dead?" Ulric asked.

"Yes. Felice Stephens was found dead two days ago. Her body was found dumped in the Puget Sound. I'd have been here sooner, but she took a while to identify. We know she worked here. We know she dated Keith. What can you tell me that we don't know?"

Keith started hyperventilating. Ulric got up from his chair, and in one smooth motion put Keith's head between his knees.

"You'll be all right. Just breathe." It was nearly paternal, and caught Lilah off guard after the scene in the bar.

"I'm sorry the news is so traumatizing Mr. Richmond. I'm afraid you need to hear all of it. You too, Ulric. If we're lucky, maybe the two of you can help me." Lilah's voice softened. It was hard to sound detached with Richmond's head between his legs. There was real pain there, and Lilah felt sorry for what she was about to do. She had to treat them both like suspects.

"When was the last time either of you saw her?"

"I'm not sure. I don't always interact with every employee." Ulric was still holding Keith's head down.

"Is that because she was human?" Lilah hoped for shock. She was disappointed.

"No, Lieutenant, it's because I'm a busy man. This isn't my only business."

"Really?"

"Does that really surprise you? Let me check payroll." Ulric walked back behind his desk, while Keith sat up, and blinked rapidly at Lilah.

"I last saw her about three weeks ago. I thought she'd broken up with me, and was just staying away because she couldn't face me. We'd had a fight. The things I called her. I mean, I never thought...oh God!" He put his head between his knees again.

"Here is it," Ulric pulled something up on his computer, "Yes, she last clocked in three weeks ago, almost exactly. Hmmm....odd?"

"What's odd?"

"She never clocked out."

Keith's eyes were red and puffy when he looked up again.

"Lieutenant Evans, how did she die?" His voice shook, and Lilah didn't think Richmond could handle the truth. A truth that was being kept out of the paper, and off line. Looking at him, she sighed.

"Ms. Stephens died horribly. At first, we thought she'd been shot in the face, which obliterated her features." Keith kept his eyes on Lilah. He wanted the truth.

"Because of who you are, I'm going to share her manner of death. If I find out either of you lie to me on this, there will be hell to pay." Every now and then a good cliché came in handy. Lilah lied, just a little bit. The police often used every measure they had, as long it as it was legal, to get information. This was no different.

"Ms. Stephens was mauled. It looks, at first glance, as though some wild animal jumped her in the city, and then threw her in the Sound. But it wasn't just any wild animal. She smelled distinctly of...well, everyone here. She smelled like wolf."

Keith jumped out of his chair, and started pacing.

"You can't think one of us did this?!?"

"I can think a lot of things. After all, I don't know you, or your pack. I don't know what you'd do. But the fight I just had? Tells me it's more than possible."

Ulric stayed calm behind his desk. "Keith, sit back down." It was an order that the lanky man followed it without question.

"Now, Lieutenant Evans, I can understand why it'd be easy to place at our feet," his voice was placating, "but not my wolves. We don't hurt or hunt humans. Especially not those we've taken under our protection. Keith here, he was dating Felice, and she worked for us. If nothing else, we want to find the person responsible as much as you do. She was as close to one of us a human can be."

"I doubt that," Lilah murmured. "Let's say for the sake of argument it wasn't you or your pack. Is there another pack in the area? There is no doubt that Ms. Stephens was killed by a werewolf.. Now, you tell me your pack would never do such a thing. I assume you have someone else you'd want me to investigate?" These guys could easily attempt to scape goat someone else.

"Lieutenant, you're not even supposed to know of our existence, and now you want me to tell you of others?"

"Unless you'd like to be booked on an accessory charge, yes." She was bluffing, but hoped Ulric didn't know that.

"Fine," he sighed "There are no other packs within two hundred miles of here. Mine is larger than you see here, but again, none of my people would, or could do this. They take an oath." Ulric took a deep breath.

"The other possibility is that we have some rogue wolves in the area. One who is unaffiliated, and has no one to be accountable to. That's always more dangerous."

"Would you know if there were rogue wolves in what seems to be your territory?"

"I'd like to think so. But even the greatest can be fooled. I'll look into it, and I'll let you know if I find anything." That was probably the closest thing Lilah was going to get to a promise to be let into the affairs of werewolves.

"Thank you Ulric, Keith. I'm terribly sorry for your loss." Lilah stood to leave.

"Can either of you tell me about the synthetic street drug Rainbow?"

The shock on Keith's face was in direct contrast to the stoicism of Ulric's. They'd heard of it.

"Is that somehow involved in this case?" Ulric asked mildly.

"This one. And a second homicide that also had all the earmarks of werewolf." Lilah sat back down.

"Plus, I've seen Rainbow in action. One person just acted wildly out of character, while another clawed her own eyes out, rather than look at me. There is more to it than a hallucinogen."

"You need to know two things about us, Lieutenant. We are a lot of things, but none of the pack would get involved in illegal drugs. That's the fast track to attention that we don't need." Lilah looked at Keith while Ulric was talking, and realized he'd gotten paler. There was something going on behind Ulric's back.

"The second? I may seem warm and cuddly. But if any of my Pack had anything to do with this, murder or drugs, they'll answer to me. And then maybe I'll send them to you."

Lilah understood the concept of pack structure, though she was new to werewolves. If one of her officers did something dumb, dangerous, or overstepped their authority, she'd be the first to reprimand them. She stood to leave again.

"If I were you, Ulric. I'd start with him." She jerked her thumb toward Keith. "Here's my card. Call anytime." She handed it to Ulric, and left. Lilah wasn't done with them, but she decided to let the death, and the news of Rainbow sit with them. Just for a while.

Lilah headed home, aching slightly from the fight, and tired beyond words.

Chapter Fourteen

There was a faint ringing. Not enough for Lilah to open her eyes. The ringing got louder, pulling her out of the warm comfort of sleep. Someday, she was going to have to learn how to set ringtones on her Smartphone. For now though, it was the average ring, and it wasn't stopping. Looking around with her half-conscious self, she slid out of bed, and to the floor. Her phone was in her pants pockets.

"Evans" she growled in to the phone.

"Did I wake you Lieutenant?" It was her boss, Captain Dave Burton. Lilah squinted at the microwave clock. She'd slept nearly twelve hours.

"Yes, but it was time. What is up, Captain?"

"There's another body. You've been requested, and I agree. I haven't been to the crime scene, but I have reports from the first on scene. There is something hinky about this one. Right up your alley."

"I'll be there. Detective Davies is checking on leads for the first body. Where am I going?"

"Pike Place Market, under the sky bridge on Western Ave, around 1500 block."

"Sir, you still haven't said. Is this homicide related to my current case?"

"I don't know. Possibly. That is one of the things I want you to tell me. Get on it Lieutenant."

"Okay, I'm on my way." Her boss hung up without saying goodbye.

It was already getting dark enough for her to move about unhindered. By the time she got to the body, it'd be dark enough.

Lilah pulled on the pants she'd taken the phone out of, a clean shirt, her shoulder holster with her Sig Saur 911, and her black trench coat. She headed out to the tunnels. There was an exit just south of the Market. The hidden tunnels and underground bits of city were her favorite things about Seattle.

Chapter Fifteen

Lilah made it to the scene and started to duck under the yellow police tape. As usual her badge was in her pocket.

"I'm sorry ma'am, this is a police only area." It was a uniformed officer she didn't recognized. Lilah decided to test him. One way to find out how much information the rookie was giving to the general public.

"Oh my. A real crime, right here. What happened officer?" She tried to put some worry into her voice.

"Ma'am, we're not allowed to talk about it."

"Please, I drive by here every day on my way to work. Can't you tell me a little something?"

The officer, who hadn't looked that stern to begin with, face softened.

"I'm still sorry ma'am. Watch the news. I'm sure there will be information on there tonight."

Lilah couldn't take it anymore. He was soft-hearted, but not weak.

"What is your name, officer?"

"Officer Perez, ma'am. If you could go wait…"

"Nice to meet you, Officer Perez." Lilah showed her badge, "I'm Lieutenant Lilah Evans, and you, Officer Perez, are keeping me from my crime scene." She let herself in under the tape, and turned back to him. "And it's always Sir, when meeting a superior officer."

"Yes ma...Sir."

"You did a good job. I've got my eye on you." She graced him with a smile, and then hurried to the flashing lights ahead. As she got closer, there were more uniformed officers, and at least one detective wearing her badge on a lanyard, at the scene itself.

"Oh my, what is going on here?" Lilah again tried to pass as a civilian, to test them, but also, sometimes in this job, she had to make your own fun. Lilah preferred it to be fun, but deep down she knew it could go the other way. Two of the uniforms raised eyebrows, but said nothing. The detective turned, and gave her angry gray eyes. She was a taller woman, mid-thirties, blond and fair of complexion, even at night. Lilah had never seen her before, and she knew by sight, anyone who out ranked her.

"Ma'am," there was that word again, "this is a crime scene. You shouldn't even be back here. I'm going to tear a new one in whoever let you in." Her voice was a bit gruff, like she'd quit cigarettes, but no one had told her throat yet.

"You mean Officer Friendly back there? He was very nice."

The unknown detective turned on her heels, grabbed Lilah's arm and started walking back that way. The detective should not lay a hand on a civilian in such a way. It pissed Lilah off.

"Number one: you're going to want to let go of me now. If I were your average Joe on the street, this would play bad to any press outside." The detective let Lilah go so hard, the only thing keeping her upright was preternatural ability, though to make a point, Lilah stumbled back.

"Number two: you could just have caught a brutality charge for the SPD." Now the other detective's eyes held worry.

"Number three: Officer Perez did a great job of keeping me out, until he couldn't. And that is number four." Lilah badged her.

"I'm Lieutenant Lilah Evans. And you are?" She asked, her voice pure ice.

The other detective decided to play a bluff of her own.

"You didn't introduce yourself at my crime scene; instead you came in playing games, while I obviously have work to do. What kind of Lieutenant are you?"

"There were uniformed officers that recognized me immediately. I have a right to check the integrity of my crime scene, using any methods I deem necessary. You know what? It normally doesn't involve manhandling anyone. As to what kind of Lieutenant I am, ask around. One more chance, who the hell are you?" Lilah watched the other detective stiffen. She was obviously used to giving the orders, not taking them.

"I'm Detective Selene Dennis. I work Vice."

"So you work with Hunter. Ask him, he knows who I am. And this is my crime scene, I was requested."

"Yeah, by Hunter. Over my head." She went to sullen quickly.

"So you're holding a grudge that Homicide was called in? Or that another female detective was called in?"

"Both ma...sir. I'd been following up on this man for weeks, a suspected supplier of a new synthetic hallucinogen out there. His suicide is gumming up the works."

"Your concern for your fellow man is touching." Her sarcasm was lost on the other officer.

"I'm willing to bet that there is at least one person here, who doesn't think it's a suicide. Since I don't know who you have up there, I can't hazard a guess. What if we walk back up there, and start over? Hi, I'm Lieutenant Lilah Evans, homicide. And you?"

"Detective Selene Dennis. Vice."

"Very good, let's go see our body before it gets up and walks out on its own." Lilah could see that she and Detective Dennis weren't going to be fast friends. Dennis just didn't get her humor.

Walking to the scene she noticed a couple huddled together in a door way. They were holding each other, crying. Lilah pegged them immediately as witnesses.

"Dennis, have you sent anyone to question the witnesses?"

"That's Detective Dennis. What witnesses?" Lilah stopped walked and stared at the younger woman.

"Please, please tell me you're joking, *Detective*," the emphasis on the title showed her displeasure with Dennis. She stopped walking to look at Lilah.

"Why would I joke about that Lieut...Sir?" Lilah shook her head.

"You were aware that there are witnesses, right?"

"No one was on the overpass that we're aware of." It came out sullen. Detective Selene Dennis did not like being questioned.

"What about anyone under it?"

"What are you talking about? How would you know if there was anyone under the overpass. You just got here!" Anger simmered in Dennis' voice.

"And yet." Lilah sighed. "Look to your right. See the couple crying in that alcove? I'd bet you a week's worth of Krispy Kreme donuts that they saw something." Perpetuating stereotypes was a hobby of Lilah's. Detective Dennis looked over and paled slightly in the dark. She turned to snag the first uniform she saw.

"Go get their statement Riggs." Detective Dennis snarled. Riggs took off toward the couple in a slow run.

"Wow. Is that how you treat your subordinates? Perhaps Detective is too high a rank for you." Lilah believed deeply that you only spoke harshly to those under you when they deserved it.

"You are a bitch!" Selene Dennis turned on her heels, and got into Lilah's face.

"Excuse me?" Lilah kept her voice mild, but did not step back. The officers who recognized Lilah turned to watch.

"You heard me, sir," she spat her words, "You're a bitch. This is my crime scene, and you've done nothing but come in and throw your weight around. Why are you here anyway? It's a suicide connected to vice. That's my jurisdiction!" Lilah looked her straight in the eye. Selene Dennis must have seen the dark and empty that showed in mirrors. Sometimes Lilah was so angry she could feel them go dark, which caused the other officer to stumble away.

"I'm going over this one more time with you, Dennis. Then, you are either going to help me, or get the fuck out of my way. As of now, there is no proof that this is a suicide. In Homicide, and the police department in general, it's never a suicide until it's been investigated and found not to be anything else. As it is, a dead body that came off the overpass walkway. You assume he jumped. That's just bad police work. Especially since you spoke to no witnesses, and you didn't see the jump. You've been rude to me, to the uniformed officers, and honestly, to the dead man up there. This isn't about you, or me. This is about him. And if you can't pull up your pants, and play nice, I'll have you removed from my crime scene, and written up. Are we clear?" Lilah barely held in her rage as she spoke.

"Crystal, sir." Some of the fight had gone out of the detective's voice. Her eyes swam with anger, but she held it in check.

"Now, we're going to look at a body. Then we're calling the ME." With that, Lilah turned and walked to the body.

Chapter Sixteen

"Shit!" Lilah knew exactly who she was looking at.

"What, sir?" Detective Dennis was trying to be cordial, or at least, slightly respectful.

"This is the man you've been following for distribution of Rainbow?"

"I never told you the name of the drug." Dennis went from respectful to suspicious.

"Just answer the question." Lilah looked at the dead man, and knew it was no suicide.

"Yes, we'd been watching him."

"You didn't watch him closely enough." Lilah sighed. "Poor Keith Richmond. He'd had quite a shock this week, but I'm pretty sure it didn't drive him to this." Lilah bent down and started examining the body. There were signs of a fall, mostly superficial. Scrapes, bruises, and the occasional contusion. But the only visible wound that bled, was a somewhat minor head wound. What really caught Lilah's eye though, was blood seeping through Richmond's shirt, at heart level. Richmond reeked of more blood than was obvious at the scene.

"Tell me what you see, Detective Dennis."

"A jumper, like I said. Look at the head wound; he must have landed on it. Obvious cause of death."

"He didn't die of a head wound. In fact, it's pretty minor. Would you like to try for the bonus round?" Lilah's snark held no bounds.

"You don't know what you're talking about. The ME hasn't even showed yet. It's all speculation."

"Is it, Detective Dennis? I'm going to guess that the dead aren't your specialty. So look here, I'm going to show you cause of death." Lilah snapped on her black nitrile gloves, and lifted Keith Richmond's shirt.

"I'd say the cause of death was obviously coronary. Or, if you prefer, the lack anything coronary." She watched as Dennis bend over and inspect the wound.

"It looks like someone punched through his chest and dug his heart out." Bewilderment filled Detective Dennis' voice.

"Yes, yes it does. So, would you like to revise your theory?" Lilah was trying to be nice.

"It's not suicide."

"No. No it isn't. Time to call in the ME, don't you think?"

"Well, this blows my case all to hell." Detective Dennis' concern for human life was touching.

"Maybe. But right now, this isn't about your case."

"You're right, ok? I know you're right, and I've acted like an ass the whole time you've been here. Do you know how hard it is to get a promotion as a woman in vice?"

Gwendolyn Jensen-Woodard

"So you're bucking for Lieutenant, is that it? Too damned bad! If you can't run a simple case, you're not getting the new badge. And if you're hoping for Captain after that, you may need a career change. Right now, I'm not sure you're even getting to keep the badge you've got. As for, do I know it's hard? Yes, I damned well do. After all, I have tits too. Now go call the ME before I decide to throw you out of my crime scene!" Lilah had enough. Some people should never join the force, and from everything she could see, Detective Selene Dennis was one of them.

Chapter Seventeen

The M.E. arrived at the scene more quickly than Lilah expected. Then again, her focus was on the crime scene on the street. Her next move was to check out the overpass. But she wanted to see the M.E. first. Lilah wondered if Doctor Drusilla Collins ever slept.

"Doctor Dru, over here." The Medical Examiner turned, and gave Lilah a smile as she made her way over.

"I figured, since I started this case with you, Lilah, that I'd see it through. What have we got? First rumor was suicide."

Lilah scowled. "If you talked to Detective Selene Dennis, disregard everything she said."

"Oh, I don't know Lilah. I believe you can be a bitch." Lilah looked shocked for a moment, and then started laughing. Dru joined her. Sometimes the level of horror is so high, that laughter kept the nightmares of the day away.

"You got that right," Lilah smiled. "This is Keith Richmond. He was Dennis' suspect in the Rainbow case. I spoke to him recently. I'm convinced he wasn't the pusher of Rainbow, but he was Felice Stephens' boyfriend. He took the news of her death very hard. Call it a hunch, but I don't think he was involved." She didn't add that the head of the local werewolf pack had promised bad things for any pack member he found to be involved with Felice Stephens death, or Rainbow. Lilah knew she'd have to go see Ulric after this. It wasn't a meeting she was relishing.

"I was also told this was a suicide. That's the most ridiculous thing I've heard today." Dru waved vaguely at the dead man with her gloved hands.

"It doesn't take much to see he'd been in a fight, and I'm guess that blood stain on his shirt is hiding a hole where his heart should be."

"I hate to say it, but you're right. Richmond is now our third victim. I think we have a serial killer on our hands." Lilah felt weary, and annoyed. How many other people were going to suffer a violent, horrible death before she finds the murderer? She knew better than to blame herself, but she did   anyway.
"Doc, you okay down here? I need to inspect the pedestrian overpass."

"I'll be fine. The dead don't tend to get up and walk away. Go, find evidence. I'll take care of Mr. Richmond now." Dru smiled at Lilah. It held a tinge of sadness.

"Ok. Yell if you need anything." Lilah smiled back. It was later than she expected, well past midnight. That gave her a few more good hours of investigating.

Up on the over pass, a different story was definitely being told. There was far too much blood for a suicide (which a jumper, usually leaves none of). In fact there was a nice pool in the middle that was likely where the heart was torn out. After checking around her, Lilah sniffed at it. Two strong smells of lycanthrope, and hearts blood. Richmond died right here. There were also signs of a heated fight. Keith

Richmond did not go quietly into that good night. He fought for his life. There were claw marks obscuring the inner walls around the death site, blood that didn't seem to be in the right place to be Richmond's, cracks to the ceiling, and gouges in the walk way. The city of Seattle was going to have to foot the bill for the damage, and for once Lilah was glad she didn't have to be part of the conversation. She took another sniff of the heart's blood, and was able to ascertain enough differences to tell that the blood in one of the claw marks was definitely from a different werewolf. Lilah collected the blood evidence. Took pictures of the entire thing, and make her way back down below the overpass.

"Doc, I'm glad you're here. I found a bloody mess upstairs, literally. I took some evidence of the blood in different areas of the overpass." Lilah signed the chain of evidence, and then handed them to Dru.

"Glad you caught me, Detective." She signed her name as well. "We were just about to head to the hospital. Tell me this, were two people killed up there?"

"I don't think so, but there was a hell of a fight. We should have the blood of the murderer."

After the doctor closed the ME van, and was certain no one could hear her: "Your kind of fight? Which means DNA I can't use?"

Lilah sighed, and nodded. "Not my people, but yes, my world."

"Awesome." Lilah was pretty sure that Dr. Dru meant the exact opposite of 'awesome'.

"I'll find out what I can doctor. This isn't over yet, but I'm definitely going to stop it. Trust me. This will end."

"Lilah, right now, you're the only one I trust. I'll feel better when these murders and Rainbow are done with."

"You said it." Lilah turned, and started walking toward the pier. There was a bar, she really had to revisit. Part of her hoped no one there was involved. The other part hoped she could take them down right now. Deep down, she knew nothing was ever that easy.

Chapter Eighteen

The night was full around her, as she made her way back to *BeBe's*. Tonight it was like a siren song, something that promises nothing but magic and power but could deliver nothing but a life close to death. Even so, she had to stop and feel it around her, soft like a black cat, with an air of mystery. She used a vampire power earlier, without meaning to, in scaring Selene Davis. The night reacted to that, to her magic and the darkness that lived just under her skin. It was a living organism, wanting her to do it again. To pull it all in, and let her darkness go. For a moment, just one, Lilah wanted to give in. To become the darkness, losing herself in the process.

"No," Lilah whispered to the night, "no!" Taking a deep breath of the cool air, she shook herself out of it.

"I will never give in. Do you HEAR ME?" Lilah screamed. The few pedestrians in the area scurried away faster. She looked and sounded crazy, angry and scared. No one wants to deal with that in the dark.

Lilah felt the night recede, knowing finally, that it was alive. She let it get too close this time, felt it pull at her soul. Lilah tried to shake off the fear and longing as she continued walking toward *Bebe's*. Lilah vowed to be more careful in the future, not letting lose the powers that lead to the dark, which waited to engulf her, to take her and leave something else in her wake.

Lilah sighed in relief as the faded blue and white sign appeared in front of her. She'd made it to the bar. They wouldn't be happy to see her, but right now, she was happy to see them. Lilah pushed her way into the bar, and took a look around. Her eyes didn't need to adjust to the light, but it was always best for people to think they did.

Fenris was behind the bar once again. He must have healed from their earlier fight already. Lilah walked up to the bar, ignoring the patrons and gave Fenris her best, shiniest smile.

"Good to see you again, Fenris. Is the boss in, I need to talk to him."

Fenris turned dark eyes to her. They proclaimed they hadn't forgotten anything, and he wanted another chance at her. There was a spark of defiance, for her, and for his leader that flashed through those lies. Lilah just kept smiling.

"He's not here." Fenris' voice was sullen.

"Why do I think you're lying? Shall I just go in the back and look for him?" Lilah was aware that any chatter in the taproom had stopped. They were being watched closely, but so far, no one else got up from their seats. The patrons, other wolves, waited to see how this played out.

"I said, he's not here. Leave."

"Really Fenris? Didn't we have this talk last time? I'm not here for a social call. I'm on police business. It's about Keith Richmond."

"He's not here either."

"Well Sherlock, I know that. That's why I'm here. So be a good dog, and get the boss." The shine had gone out of her

140

voice, she was tired of games. It'd already been a long night, and Fenris was pissing her off.

"What did you just say to me?"

"I didn't take you for stupid, Fido. I said, go get your master like a good dog." There was an audible gasp from the other wolves. Fenris started to walk around the bar, toward her and not the back.

"Do you really want to do this again? Last time I busted your leg. This time, I won't stop there." He continued walking toward her. She tried a different tactic.

"Ulric, oh Ulric." Lilah used a loud, sing song voice, "I need to talk to you, and your guard dog won't let me. This is a police matter, and taking him downtown would hurt all of you. ULRIC!" Lilah was bluffing about taking Fenris downtown, but that was something they didn't need to know. She heard someone moving about in the office in the back, and a white, hot burst of power emanating toward the bar.

"What the hell is going on?" Ulric growled. Perhaps she'd woken him up.

"This...person wanted to see you. I told her you weren't in. She insulted me several times before calling for you. I was going to throw her out, personally."

Ulric scowled at him. "Didn't you learn a damn thing last time?" He turned his eyes to Lilah, "And what else do you need?"

"I'm sorry to bother you, Ulric. But I need to talk to you about Keith Richmond and I'd rather not do it out here. If you can make him heel, I think Fenris needs to be in this too."

"Bleddyn, come take the bar." A man she hadn't seen before, wearing ripped jeans and an old Ramones tee-shit stood up, his lanky frame slightly hunched. He slid behind the bar like he belonged there, and started wiping it down with a rag. Bleddyn never once looked their way.

"Welsh this time, nice."

Ulric gave her hard eyes. Maybe it wasn't the time to talk about the origin of their names. Lilah took note of it.

"Fenris, you're with us. Oh, and Lieutenant Evans? Please stop with the dog jokes. You offended everyone in here, me included."

"For that I'm sorry. I only intended to offend Fenris. He refused to tell you I was here. This is important. Believe me, you want to talk to me tonight. I'll try not to do it again."

"Good, because you don't want to fight me." His power gave her a small slap, which stung a tiny bit. Perhaps she was done insulting the wolves. It was hard to say, sometimes she even surprised herself.

They made their way back into the spotless office. Well, almost spotless, this time the cot in the corner had a mussed army green blanket on top. Lilah suspected Ulric didn't hear her when she first came into the bar, because he was sleeping. Ulric set himself behind the desk, and motioned to Lilah to take a seat. Fenris sat on the cot.

"Well?"

"Keith Richmond is dead." Lilah watched to see their reactions, so gave no warning or preamble.

Ulric blinked, and Fenris paled slightly.

Gwendolyn Jensen-Woodard

"Are you sure?" From Fenris.

"Would I say such a thing if I weren't? I saw his body."

"How did he die?" Ulric said quietly.

"He was murdered. I still would have come myself to tell you, but I wouldn't have made such a scene had it been a natural death. I need to know, were either of you up by the Market this afternoon?"

"No." They said it in unison. Neither felt like a lie.

"Ulric, I think I can trust you. Fenris, I have no idea."

"You can trust him." Ulric's voice had a final ring. "He earned his way to being my second." Fenris would do as he was told, or face the consequences. It was good enough for her. For now.

"Keith's heart was ripped out, and he was thrown from the pedestrian overpass at the Market. There was a full on fight, with what looked to be claws in the overpass. The smell was overwhelming of two different wolves. I can't take that part back to the department, but I can bring it to you. It likely has to do with Ms. Stephens' death and once again, the hallucinogenic Rainbow. I need to know if you've found anything in your pack connected to either of those."

"I'm sorry, Detective. And I'm not. I've found nothing in my pack to connect to the death or the drug. No one in my pack would dare kill another member in such a way." Lilah raised an eyebrow, as Ulric didn't say at "wouldn't dare kill another member." He had mentioned something about hierarchy and pack rule the last time they met. Another problem, for another day.

143

Night Hues

"There was no way anyone could have done it without your knowledge?"

"Risking my wrath? I don't think any of my pack would do so. I may seem like a nice guy, but pack rules are followed." Fenris nodded from the cot. He was a badass, and he followed Ulric without challenge.

"If you do find anything out…" She let it hang.

"You'll be my second call." Same answer as last time. Lilah figured that was the best she was going to get. Richmond, like Felice Stephens, was one of their own.

Chapter Nineteen

The night was tinged with the pink light of dawn. Lilah made her way home, wondering if there was a difference in werewolf packs. Were they all like Ulric's, with the rigid pack structure that she still didn't entirely understand? Or could it be something different? Could unaffiliated wolves, join a new pack? She wished she knew.

Lilah had just reached her door when the phone rang. It was always about timing with these things. She fumbled for it as she walked into her apartment and shut the door.

"Evans."

"It's Davies. I have a report on Stephens' residence. I heard you'd been embroiled in another dead body, but no one requested me on scene. So I figured we could talk now." He seemed annoyed. She should have called him.

"I'm sorry. You should have been there. I got to dress down a Vice cop. That was the fun part." It really hadn't been.

"I heard. You're the talk of the force. Cops like gossip as much as the next person. It keeps us entertained. Did you actually slap her into submission?"

"Is that what they're saying? I'm not surprised, some reports read like fiction." Now she was joking. "I didn't touch her. I just threated to have her busted down to traffic." Not entirely true, but closer than slapping. "You'd have hated her."

"Sounds like it. Okay, now that we're done with social hour, let's talk about the case."

Lilah closed her door, and flopped on her couch. Weary was the best way to describe her current state. Still, work before sleep.

"Okay, what have you got?"

"Stephens' neighbors said she was a nice girl. They sometimes saw her with a guy, but they never heard anything out of the ordinary. It's not the best building, but there is a little sound proofing. No one could say a bad word about her. She was nice, she sometimes helped with doors and carrying things. Hell, she brought one of them homemade cookies after he broke his leg." Davies let out a sigh.

"How was her apartment?"

"Clean. Not a sign of a struggle anywhere. Everything was in its place. Even her bed was made. It was sad, Lilah. Like her apartment was just waiting for her return."

"Did you see any sign that she might be using drugs?"

"No. Nothing that would indicate drug use. Why, was her death drug related?"

"It seems so. Doctor Dru found a synthetic hallucinogenic in the toxicology screen. Street name Rainbow."

"Damn. But that can't be what killed her. No drug mauls its taker. At least, not on the outside."

"True. We're still working on cause of death. Doctor Dru thought maybe it was a shot gun blast to the face." That was the story she and Drusilla agreed on. Lilah didn't like lying to her partner, but still felt she had no choice.

"Ok. If you say so."

"You sound like you don't believe me." Lilah tried to sound offended.

"Since we started working together, I've seen some strange things. Stephens, Schaffer, and more. But, you're lead. I bow to your analysis." At that moment, Lilah knew she'd get no better answer. Still, better he stay safe and out of her world. She didn't want to get him killed. He was a pain the ass sometimes, but he was her pain in the ass.

"Thank you." She said simply, closing the matter. "The crime scene today, another mauling. With the heart missing from the scene. The difference this time, Rainbow wasn't found in his system. Keith Richmond was his name."

"Felice Stephens' boyfriend?"

"One and the same."

"Well, this is a fine mess." A Laurel and Hardy reference.

"How old are you Davies? That quote seems a little out of your age range."

"What, you think men in their thirties can't have some class? My grandfather loved everything from early films to '70's television. I watched with him."

"Ah." Lilah had nothing else to say to that. Davies changed the subject.

"Do we have any suspects in these murders?"

"There are a few leads I'm following. Nothing concrete yet. I'll let you know when I have more information. Right now, I think it's time for sleep. Meet you at the station around 6pm. We'll talk more then."

"You got it. Sleep well, and don't let the bedbugs bite." This time, Davies hung up first.

Lilah sighed, heading for the fridge. It wasn't bedbugs she feared would bite her.

Chapter Twenty

The SPD was still bustling at 6:00pm. It was nice to know someone worked while she slept. Lilah made her way to her office. This time, there was transient sitting on the bench, trying to beat up her officers. There was a smattering of "Hi Lieutenant's" as she came through, but no one needed her attention right away. Davies was already there, at his desk. He gave a random wave, and squinted at his computer, working on his report.

Lilah sighed and closed the door to her office. She loved being a police officer. She hated paperwork. The first the thing she noticed was a report on Barney Linner. Lilah knew most of what was written in the report. It was determined he didn't kill anyone, which was good. There was also a tox screen. She scanned it, taking note of one thing "unknown hallucinogenic". Though she was certain he'd been on Rainbow, it was nice to get conformation. Setting the file aside, she woke her computer up, and entered some insane password the IT department had given her. Pulling up the report document she started with the Schaffer case. She'd barely gotten into it, when the phone buzzed.

"Evans."

"You and Davies report to my office." Captain Burton hung up. Not sure why they were being summoned, she swore softly and left her office.

"Davies, with me." He stood without complaint.

"What's up Evans?"

"The Captain wants us, now."

Davies joined her walking to the Captain's office.

As always, the Captain's assistant, Dolores, was at her desk. It was past 6pm. Maybe she worked when the Captain did. It was part of the mystery of having desk job, and Lilah didn't know how it worked. Still, it was nice to see Dolores. Dolores was shorter than Lilah, perhaps 5'1", and had bright red hair that came from a bottle. It was an amazing dye job, looked natural. Dolores always had a ready smile, no matter the situation.

"Hi Lilah, hi Allen. The Captain is expecting you, go right in." Her voice was bouncy, which was likely in contrast to what they'd find in the office.

"Thanks Dolores."

Being the senior member of their little team, Lilah went first. After all, it was only fair. Davies was right behind her.

"Get in here, and close that door." Captain Dave Burton was a tall man, with short cropped white hair, and ruddy complexion. His brown eyes looked drawn, and he wasn't smiling. Lilah and Davies stood out of respect.

"Okay you two, what the hell is going on?" Lilah wondered if he was getting grief from up high.

"Sir, can you be more specific?" Lilah spoke up for herself and Davies.

"Yes, I certainly can. What is going on with these bizarre murders? I haven't had a full report from either of you.

"I was working on mine when you called us in, Sir. We can give you a report now, if you'd like." Lilah wished she'd done the paperwork earlier.

"Of course I'd like a report now. I didn't just call you in here for giggles. Evans you first, then Davies." His voice was gruff, with a hint of frustration.

"Yes sir. The first body was found near Pier 70, in the water. She'd been shot in the face, making identification difficult. Name was Felice Stephens, a waitress at *Bebe's*, a bar down by the water. And she was missing her heart. This is the thread that connects all the bodies.

"The second body was found in his apartment, and it looked like he was ravaged by a large dog, or wolf. His heart was also missing. But unlike Felice who worked a subsistence job, the second victim was a partner at *Schaffer, Carson and Retan Designs*, an architectural firm. As far as we can tell, they never met, or socialized in the same circles.

"Victim number three, Keith Richmond did have a tie to the first victim. They both worked at *Bebe's* and dated. When interviewed it was obvious Richmond knew nothing of Stephens' death. Again the cause of death was the same, removal of the heart. The circumstances around his death were slightly different however. He seemed mauled in a similar way as the other two, but the crime scene shows there was a terrible fight. After, his body was dumped over the edge of the pedestrian overpass at the Pike Place Market. Someone tried, and failed to make it look like a suicide.

"The first two victims had one more thing in common; they both had the hallucinogenic Rainbow in their systems. We're not sure what it does," Lilah hated lying to her boss, but there was nothing else she could do, "but a few side effects seem to be changing the person's eye color, violence, and of course hallucinations."

"Hallucinations? Is that what happened to Gracie Roman while in Hunter's custody? They said she looked at you, and clawed her eyes out."

"Yes sir. I don't know what the drug mad her see, but it must have been horrific." If they hadn't been in the Captain's office, Lilah knew Davies would have a smart remark to that.

"Detective Davies, have you got anything to add? Suspects perhaps?" The frustration in his voice was more evident.

"So far, no Sir. We've searched Stephens' and Schaffer's apartments. Nothing came up on either. Other than the damage to Schaffer's home, which happened at the time of his death. It looked like claw marks, but it could have been an axe or hatchet of some kind. We couldn't find enough to link it to a specific weapon, though hatchet seems the most likely."

The Captain sighed.

"I'm getting heat from the Mayor's office. They want these murders solved as soon as possible. He's is afraid of tourism being effected. Especially after the Pike Place incident. Which reminds me, Lieutenant, I got a call from Detective Selene Dennis in Vice. She felt you were disrespectful to her in front of the uniformed officers, that you threatened her, and that you reprimanded her. Is that what happened?"

"Yes sir, and more. Dennis made a mess of her crime scene. She assumed, without even looking, that it was suicide and was more angry because she thought Richmond was her

Rainbow connection. It didn't occur to her to check the overpass, or to talk to witnesses. On top of that, she showed no respect when talking to me. I had to teach her a lesson, Sir, in decorum and police procedures." Lilah shook her head.

"In other words, you gave her a verbal boot to her ass?" He gave a slight grin.

"Yes sir. And I'd do it again. Homicide should have been called in immediately, but Dennis was looking for the path to promotion, and therefore broke several protocols. She had it coming, Sir."

"Yes, I see that she did. That complaint will end here. I see nothing inappropriate with your behavior." The Captain sobered.

"You two need to get back out there. Knock on doors again, visit the bar, do what you have to do, but get an answer, and close this damned case. Hopefully before more people die!"

"Yes Sir!" They answered in unison.

Chapter Twenty-One

Detective Allen Davies stopped her as they were walking down the hall. He pulled her into one of the few quiet nooks in the precinct. Sitting on a light blue chair, he motioned for her to do the same.

"What is up?" Lilah sat.

"That's what I want to ask you. I know how good you are at this. Finding clues, causes of death, suspects. So why aren't you doing that now? Or are you just not sharing? I'm your partner, damn it! What aren't you telling me?" Davies was visibly upset.

"I have nothing concrete. Just vague suspicions. That's why I needed you on the apartments, and the canvassing. Trying to find any actual evidence we can use. After all, how did a large dog or wolf get into Schaffer's building? Who fought with Richmond? I'm counting on you to find the last pieces of the puzzle. I've been to *Bebe's*, and yes there are people there capable of hurting someone. Do I think they did? No idea.

"So I'm not keeping anything from you. I'm counting on you to help round out the case and to help find the actual bad guys." Lilah hated lying to her partner again. Of course, she couldn't tell him the truth. It'd just put him in danger, and that she couldn't do.

Davies sighed. "Okay, I get it. Just tell me what you do have something. We're both swinging here."

"I promise. And no matter what happens, I won't let you swing."

"With all due respect, yes you will. I'm your partner, and this is our case. One of us takes a hit, we both do." Lilah knew he was wrong, but let him believe it. It was actually nice of him. "If you say so. Now, let's get these reports done, before dawn breaks."

Davies smirked, "I always wondered, do you turn into a pumpkin?"

"Smart ass!" She laughed a bit, knowing they were back to the usual routine. Davies went back to his desk, and she to her office.

It was nearly 5:30am when Lilah hit send, her paperwork flying in 1's and 0's to Captain Burton's office. Looking outside, it was still dark enough for her to get home with no problems. As she left, she noticed Davies' desk was empty. He finished before she did. Which was good, she wanted him to get some rest. The precinct was still fairly quiet, which made for an easy getaway.

Since it wasn't light yet, Lilah left her car in the parking garage, and made her way to the nearest tunnel. Piece after piece was being condemned because cave-ins and general safety concerns. That was not something Lilah worried about. She could hold up a beam, or dig out of rubble without a thought, and she could walk through anything so lightly, it was unlikely she'd disturb anything. Lilah found it fascinating, seeing pieces of a different time, and a different world. One she'd seen some of when it was still standing.

Lilah took the shortest route to her apartment, feeling the stress of the few days. It was time to eat, and relax. She barely heated up her steak, when she threw it on a plate and flopped onto the couch. Lilah was about to take her first bite, when someone knocked on the door.

"Who is it?" She yelled from the couch.

"Fenris." What the hell? What the hell could he want, they weren't exactly movie buddies. Plus, being a police officer, her address was unlisted for a reason.

"Hold on." Setting the steak on the coffee table, she rose and opened the door.

"Lieutenant Evans? May I come in, please" He wasn't the gruff, angry man she'd met at *Bebe's*, instead he sounded a bit scared.

"Are we going to fight?"

"No. I'm here for your help." He sounded sincere.

"Fine, come in." She opened the door wide enough to let him in, and sat down on the couch again. "Forgive me; you caught me in the middle of dinner."

Fenris shut the door behind him, but stayed standing.

"That seems a little rare."

"The rarer the better. But you didn't come here to discuss my diet. What's going on?" Lilah bit into the steak while he talked.

"There is a rogue werewolf in our territory. He doesn't belong here, and I'm afraid he's the one that brought in Rainbow, and that killed Keith and those other people. Ulric knows this too, and he isn't coming to you. Instead, he'll take him on himself."

"You're worried for your pack leader? He gave every intention that he could take care of anything that came his way."

"I would never talk badly about my Pack leader. In most cases he can, Lieutenant. But I'm worried this time."

"At this point call me Lilah."

"Lilah then. Ulric is strong, and quite powerful. But this interloper? He or she is on drugs, Rainbow specifically. I heard it makes many humans violent. Can you imagine what it does to werewolves? I fear that Ulric will be outmatched, that this stranger would be faster, and stronger due to the drug. Ulric can be grumpy, but in the pack structure his power is absolute. We would not function well without him. Someone would fight their way up to leader, but no one would be Ulric."

Fenris' concern certainly seemed real. There was no bravado, no anger, just worry in his voice.

"How can I help? I'm pretty sure Ulric would be pissed if he knew you came to me. Pack business and all."

Fenris sighed. "You don't know the half of it. I could be disciplined quite harshly. But it's worth it if you can save him. He's going to confront the stranger at midnight tonight, up in Freeway Park. There are parts of it even the homeless don't go in, so it'll be private. Ulric is a man of his word. I would bet the other guy isn't. So please. Please help me."

Fenris used the word please twice, leading Lilah to think Fenris was completely serious.

"Was the pack forbidden to go help?"

"Yes. He didn't want any of us hurt." That seemed odd to Lilah. What is the point of having a pack, if you don't ask for help? Having always been solitary, other than the police force, she was at a bit of a loss.

"What are you prepared to do, Fenris? Run back to the safety of *Bebe's*?"

Fenris shook his head, and she could feel a bit of power starting to roll off of him, angry and stabbing. Lilah implied he was a coward. She knew it was rude, but she needed to know.

"I'm going with you. As I said earlier, there will be repercussions for me. I don't care. Ulric's safety is my first concern. I'd make a bad second if I left him to die. I just can't do that." Fenris' eyes were full of concern. Lilah had to rethink her opinion of the man: maybe he wasn't the selfish, self-entitled werewolf she thought him to be.

"All right. We'll go together. I certainly can't take my partner; he knows nothing of this world. I'd like to keep it that way, for his safety. I heard you guys remove anyone who finds out what you are."

Fenris looked startled. "We've never done that, Lilah. After all Felice Stephens worked for us. Though it's rare that humans learn our secrets, it's happened. We may encourage them to leave town, perhaps with a threat of violence, but we don't kill humans. Ever."

Lilah would have to correct Liam Campbell the next time she saw him. It was bad business telling people that the werewolves kill humans. It made them look worse than what they were. Once this was over, she was going to cross-check everything she knew.

"Meet me here at 10 p.m.. Hopefully we can save Ulric, and stop a murderer."

"Thank you Lilah. You'll never know how much this means. See you tonight." Fenris slipped back out the door, and left Lilah to finish her steak alone.

Chapter Twenty-Two

Lilah tried to take a short nap, but the upcoming confrontation kept running through her head. She couldn't place it, but after thinking about it for hours, something felt off. Hinky. It was likely to bite her in the ass, because she just couldn't place it. Whatever is was, she hoped to fix it before someone died.

Lilah dressed similarly to her normal clothes. All black, except this time, ever her socks were black. She didn't want a flash of color giving her away. She shrugged into her vertical shoulder holster, and checked her Sig Saur 1911, before sliding it into place. She covered it with her black leather trench coat. Even the black of Lilah's hair would blend into the monochrome.

Ten o'clock came faster than she thought, startled by a knock at her door. She quickly made her way out of the bedroom and to the door.

"Well, you look...dark." Fenris looked her up and down.

"So do you." His clothes were dark shades of black and blue. It matched his skin well enough, that he'd blend into the darkness. He was even wearing dark glasses.

"Worried about the sun?"

"Nope, just have sensitive eyes. Not everyone like me does, but several do. It's a throwback gene. I think. Genetics was never my best subject."

"Ok. File that under another thing I didn't know." She paused, "Are you sure you've told me everything?" Lilah was still certain she was missing something.

"I've told you it all, Lilah. I know it's a lot, but I left nothing out." His personality was so different from the first time they met. Lilah wasn't sure if it was refreshing or creepy.

"Do you have a car?" Lilah didn't think Fenris would fit in her little white car. Which she'd left in the Seattle Police Department's parking garage. For her, it was emergency transportation, not how she got around normally.

"No, I loped here in wolf form. Think anyone saw?" Sarcasm put Lilah more at ease.

"Can we ride together then? I could walk it, but it might take a bit longer than you'd like." That was a very slight fib, she could get there quickly on her own, but it wasn't something she needed to advertise.

"Of course you can. Tonight we're a team."

"Well, let's make a good one then. Do we need anything else?"

"Nope, just us. We're pretty lethal on our own. Ready?"

"Is there a second choice? I didn't think so." She smiled at her own joke, and she thought Fenris might have cracked a smirk.

Fenris stepped out of the apartment first. Lilah closed the door, locking it. They made their way to the car, not speaking much. Lilah was surprised he drove a dark, late model Toyota Camry. She'd had him pegged as a muscle car guy.

Gwendolyn Jensen-Woodard

The tension was palpable in the car. They were heading for danger, and they both knew it. Speech seemed more like a luxury, so they spent the time in silence as they made their way to Freeway Park.

Chapter Twenty-Three

It took longer than expected to reach the park. Traffic wove the streets of Seattle as one sports game or another let out. It was 11:30pm by the time they parked. Ulric was supposed to meet this mystery werewolf at midnight.

"We need to move, if we're going to be in place in time." Lilah worried aloud.

"You're not wrong. Hopefully there is a place we can hide while waiting. If we're standing there when Ulric or the mystery werewolf shows up, nothing will go as planned." Fenris was dead serious.

"Point taken, let's go."

Lilah followed Fenris up into the park, and then through a faded path leading away from downtown, and the main park. The few people that were there seemed to avoid the direction they travelled. Perhaps it was a supernatural hotspot; humans avoided them, always feeling uneasy near one. If that was the case, she had no idea how this would affect the fight, or the other preternatural creatures. Or the humans could be feeling the darkness that was about to be there. Tonight the dark tore at her, begging to be used, to make her part of the darkness. Lilah ignored it, but couldn't block it out entirely.

"Do you feel that?" Lilah whispered to Fenris.

"The night? It's always telling me to run, to be free." Lilah always felt the opposite, that it wanted a slave to make a slave of her.

"I hope you can resist it."

"I can if you can." It was a jab, another ploy to see who was the best. The first one since he'd come to see her. This time, Lilah didn't mind. It was something else to focus on.

They walked further in, until the path started coming to an end. Lilah surmised that the end of the path was the meeting space. Trite, yet appropriate.

"This way," Fenris veered off the path, and into the trees and brush. Once they were far enough away that they could barely see the meeting spot, there was a nice flat rock. It'd make a good seat until the show started, and midnight was coming fast.

It wasn't long before footsteps could be heard coming up the path. For once Lilah was glad she didn't have to breathe (though she preferred breathing). She and Fenris watched as Ulric walked up, got to the end, and waited with his arms crossed. To Lilah, he didn't look nervous, just angry. Lilah looked up at Fenris, who was staring intently at his pack leader. It took her a moment, before realizing she'd been had. There was no unknown werewolf in the city. Just Fenris verses Ulric. She wasn't entirely sure who the murderer was, but she took a chance.

"You bastard!" She whispered. Fenris turned to her, a rictus smile on his face. His hands had started to change as he bent to grab her. Relying on her speed, she ran towards Ulric, calling his name. Lilah reached him before Fenris did.

"What are you doing here, Lieutenant?" He sounded angry, and perhaps worried.

"Fenris brought me. He's the murderer, and he's coming for you. For us!" Lilah felt frantic. She was pretty sure Fenris was on Rainbow, and had no idea how that'd affect a werewolf.

"What are you talking about? He set up the meeting between me and the murderer..." Just then Fenris burst from the trees. He was in full wolf-man, covered with dark brown fur. Since he was no longer wearing the dark glasses, Lilah could see his eyes changing colors, rainbow colors glowing from the dark face. The body came with long fangs and sharp claws.

"I lured you both here. Two assholes, one stone. I'll kill you both, and keep doing what I'm doing. I'll be pack leader of The Beasts. All of my problems will be solved once neither of you are left alive." Fenris didn't attack immediately. He gloated instead. Maybe they could use that to their advantage.

"Do you really think you can take me?" Ulric began to feel of power, smell of the forest and something wild.

"Good point. Fenris, you couldn't take me at the bar, what makes you think you can do it now?" Lilah knew it was a taunt, hoping she'd throw him off, at least a little. Instead, he answered without missing a beat.

"I wasn't on Rainbow at that moment. Haven't you figured it out yet? What this does for humans is incredible. But what it does to us is astronomic. Strength, speed, will of purpose. I'll tear out your hearts, and eat them for breakfast." He snarled the last bit.

"Oh really? I don't think mine will do you much good." Lilah laughed. She could feel Ulric changing beside her.

"I'll take that chance." Fenris growled, as he stalked toward her. Lilah often got that reaction from people. The power behind her was warm, powerful, and pissed off.

"You want a fight Fenris? You want to feel real power, not something you get from a pill, come at me. I can give you the fight of your life. A thrill you'll never find without me!" Now in full were-man form as well, Ulric was the larger of the two, in fur of white and black, his eyes a deep ice blue. From all appearances, it didn't look like a fair fight, but Lilah had seen firsthand what Rainbow did to humans. She had no doubt Fenris was not the same as the man she beat in the bar.

Fenris let out another growl, his clawed hand swiping out faster than Lilah could see. It sent her flying into the brushes behind her, landing on her back. While she was there, she could hear the fight starting. Lilah couldn't let Ulric fight Fenris alone. She got to her feet, and sped back to help him.

By the time she returned, Fenris had a rather severe gash across his face. Ulric had a few more slashes across his chest and side. Neither was slowed down by the injuries. Lilah quietly went behind Fenris.

"You don't want to play at anything resembling fair, so why should we?" Lilah whispered, and landing two hard blows to his kidney. He yelped in pain, turning away from Ulric. As he looked at her she punched him in the throat, with vampire strength. He stumbled back a few inches, but did end up on one knee.

"Haven't we been here before Fenris," she taunted, hoping to give Ulric a chance to gather his power. "I dislocated your knee last time. What do you think now?"

Fenris gave a roar, a human noise not an animal one.

"You aren't going to do anything, bitch!" Fenris, on the one knee, punched her in the stomach, knocking her down again. This time, it actually hurt. It was as though Rainbow had a similar effect as PCP. Still, she couldn't let him kill Ulric or get away. Lilah struggled again to her feet, just as Ulric struck out, his claws sinking into the other werewolf's chest, under the heart, near the lungs.

"I don't want to kill you, but you are leaving me no choice. How could you do this to the humans, to Keith, and most of all, to the pack?" Ulric held his claws in Fenris' chest as he asked.

Fenris' voice bubbled a little, but was still strong.

"Why shouldn't I? The pack? Ha! It's your pack, not mine. I came to town to take it over, being packless at the time. But you were there, and so powerful. So I fought my way up to your second. Waiting for the day that I could put you down, like the dog you really are. The rest, I did right under your nose. That should discredit you with the pack. I may not be able to go back and lead, but you'll never see them again. Great revenge, if you can get it. And I can. Ulric you're too soft. Know how I know? You should have killed me, and now you're going to die!"

Fenris stood quickly with Ulric's claws still inside of him. His movements were so fast, Ulric had no time to move, before Fenris swept downward, breaking the arm sticking from his chest.

"NO!" Lilah yell as Ulric howled. She was so surprised and strangely distraught at the break, she pulled some of the night into herself. Lilah did it without thought to her humanity or soul. With new found strength she hit Fenris in the face, her fist aimed at the air behind his head. She didn't quite have the momentum for that, but she felt his eye socket fold in upon itself, as the vitreous and blood ran out of his face and down her hands.

Fenris snarled, snapping at her arm, trying to get a good bite hold. Lilah pulled back quickly, and readied for another strike. This time Fenris was faster, pinning the hurt Ulric to the ground, claws placed in the leader's chest, right over the pack leader's heart.

"Stay down," Fenris growled at Lilah, "Unless you want to see his heart blood right now." Lilah stopped, still in the night.

"What do you want Fenris? I thought you want our hearts." Lilah talked to him, making no move closer.

"I do, more than anything I do want your hearts. But if I take his now, you'll kill me from behind. If I turn, and attack you, he'll snap my neck. So we're going to make a deal. You're going to let me go, and I'll let you both live."

"Don't do it," Ulric wheezed, due to Fenris' weight upon him, "he lies." Lilah knew that was true, she could smell the lie in the air, sour and bleak. Another perk of the night, she thought briefly. Lilah knew to keep him talking.

"Oh really? What are you terms?"

"You don't come after me, you just let me leave. I'll disappear into the night, and you'll never see me again." Lie upon lie. He'd come back, and kill them both.

He turned his face to Ulric's. "Or, if you like, I'll kill him right now and then come after you. Wherever you go, I'll be there waiting eat your heart. So make a choice."

Gwendolyn Jensen-Woodard

Lilah managed to catch Ulric's eye while Fenris was looking at him. She winked, and hoped he play along. She had a plan.

"Fine. Say I believe you. You get off of him, and head away from us. I want to see your back walking away. If you turn around, if you so much as veer off the path, I'll kill you. Don't for a second think I can't." She meant what she said, but not in that order.

"If you say so. After all, you're a cop, why would you lie? You can even watch as I go, Lilah."

"Call me Lieutenant."

"Fine, Lieutenant then. And fuck you!" He slowly slid off of Ulric, and did his best to stand straight, even with one eye and a punctured lung. "Don't follow me." He turned and started down the path. She glanced at Ulric, who had blood welling up and over his chest. He wasn't going to be able to help her. He gave her the slightest nod. Lilah nodded back, and turned toward Fenris.

She'd meant to run after him, but the night had other ideas. Her feet left the ground, and she was on him before either of them knew what happened. Lilah landed on his back, and put her hands on either side of his neck.

"This is for Dick Schaffer, Keith Richmond, Felice Stephens, Ulric and anyone you hurt while on or by distributing Rainbow."

Fenris managed to squeak "I didn't..."

"I don't care." Lilah snapped his neck in one quick movement. Fenris was in hell before he knew he was dead. As he fell, she rolled off over his head, landing in a standing position. Before her eyes, he changed back to the man she'd met back at Bebe's.

Chapter Twenty-Four

Lilah rushed back to Ulric, worried for his heath. She had aches and pains herself, but the claws hadn't touched her. Ulric lay on his back on the patch of grass at the end of the path, just where she'd left him. He was still in wolf man form, which was good. He was still alive. Lilah reached his side, and fell to her knees.

"Ulric?" His eyes fluttered open, and Lilah could see the pain leaking from them.

"My phone," his voice was weak, "dial 2. Please." Shutting his eyes again, there was no further movement. Ulric had an older phone, which wasn't locked. She hit the 2 on quick dial and waited. A sleepy voice came over the phone.

"Ulric?"

"I'm Lieutenant Lilah Evans. I'm with Ulric, and he's badly hurt. Who am I speaking with?"

"Ingrid, I'm the doctor in the pack. You're the one who dislocated Fenris' knee a while back. Where are you?"

"Freeway Park, far back into the woods. Can you find us?"

"Dear, I can find Ulric anyway, he's my pack leader. I'm not far. I have questions, but I'll ask them later. Be there in ten minutes." Ingrid hung up. Perhaps it wasn't just police who have that habit.

"Ulric, it's Lilah. I don't know if you can hear me, but I'm here. Ingrid is on her way. Fenris is dead. If you die, the asshole wins. I know you; you're a proud and strong pack leader. You can't have that!" There was no reaction, but she kept talking anyway. It was the longest ten minutes of her very long life.

Finally, she heard someone making their way down the path.

"Oh my!" It was the voice she'd heard on the phone. Ingrid must have found Fenris. She didn't stop, and continued down to Ulric and Lilah.

"What happened?" Ingrid demanded of Lilah.

"Fenris doubled crossed us. He said Ulric was meeting with the murderer," Lilah assumed the whole pack knew about the murders by now, "talked me into going to help. Then revealed himself to be the murderer. He wanted to kill us both, and take Ulric's place in the pack. We fought. Both had serious injuries. Fenris pretended he was going to leave us all alone, but we knew better. I killed him. Afterward, Ulric told me to call you, and passed out. I think his wounds are serious."

Even while Lilah explained, Ingrid was looking Ulric over, and mumbling to herself.

"Ingrid, what is going on with him?"

"The cut on his arm has bled profusely, but I'm more worried about the puncture wounds near the heart. I fear one punctured the pericardial sac causing blood to pool around his heart, inside the sac. If we can get him to change to full wolf form, which may not be possible, he'll heal. It'll be slow because this was inflicted by the claws of another wolf. But we can try."

Ingrid opened the bag she'd been carrying, and pulled out a vial and a syringe.

"What is that?"

"Epinephrine. It'll either wake him up, or kill him. But if he wakes up, he'll have that moment to change. Lilah, I can't tell you which will happen. But if we do nothing, he's going to die, and that is assured." Ingrid looked cool on the outside, except her eyes. They revealed nothing but pain.

Lilah shook her head, and flexed her fingers. She could still feel the night wrapped around them.

"Let me try something first? If it doesn't work, I'll stand back and let you jab him. Please..."

The doctor looked at Lilah for a moment, and sniffed the air. Something in it, made her give Lilah a chance.

"Do it."

Lilah leaned over Ulric, spacing her hand around the puncture wounds. Shutting her eyes, she forced the night, the magic into his body. She could see the damage in her head, could feel the tissues. The worst was around his heart, where blood had actually pooled in the sac around his heart. With a slight flick of her finger, the blood came up through the wound, saturating her hand. Ingrid watched as it soaked into Lilah's skin. Lilah didn't notice as she kept working. She wrapped the night around his heart, and used it to close the hole, like darning a sock.

Once that hole was fixed, the rest was easy. A little of her magic, and his skin knit together. As she pulled her hand away, the holes in his chest filled in and healed. Even his arm had stopped bleeding. Lilah opened her eyes, sat back on her heels, and rested. She was achy and exhausted. And strangely exhilarated.

"How did you do that? We have amazing healing skills, but I've never seen anything that even resembles what you just did. What are you?" Ingrid looked interested, but also a little afraid.

"Would you believe me, if I said I have no idea what I did?" In truth, Lilah had a little idea. But it wasn't anything she'd done before. Until tonight, she didn't know she could. Maybe she'd never be able to do it again. Maybe she didn't want to. She firmly believed it was another stain on her tarnished soul.

"I don't know. For the sake of expediency, for now, I'll believe you. But sometime, I think I'd like talking to you about it."

"Maybe we will. I have questions as well. But now isn't the time." They both turned back to Ulric.

His eyes were fluttering open. Although his wounds had healed, Ulric lost too much blood. He was weak.

"Ingrid?" Ulric whispered weakly.

"I'm here, my Thorin."

"Thorin?" A word Lilah hadn't heard in reference to Ulric.

"Pack leader." Ulric whispered, "A title I hardly use. Ingrid must be worried."

"You've lost a lot of blood, Ulric. We've got to get you to my place for an infusion. Lilah, I'm taking him to my house. Do you want to join us?"

"I can't. I have Fenris to take care of." Lilah wasn't looking forward to this.

"The pack won't want him now, do what you must." Ingrid picked Ulric up as though he weighed no more than a baby. Werewolves were stronger than Lilah had first believed.

"Lilah," Ulric croaked, "I don't know what happened, but thank you. I and my pack will not forget this."

"He's right." With that, Ingrid turned, and ran out of the park carrying her leader.

Chapter Twenty-Five

Lilah walked back to Fenris' body. Dead, he seemed so much smaller than the big man she knew him to be. He was wearing the clothes she'd met him in, and for a moment Lilah wondered where the clothes went when he changed. Perhaps she'd ask Ulric one day.

Fenris' neck was bent at an unnatural angle. She couldn't have that. Leaning down, Lilah turned his head, and snapped it slightly back the other way. She knew Doctor Drusilla Collins would find the injury upon autopsy. Lilah trusted Dru would discuss it with her, before writing her final report.

Still looking at the body, Lilah drew her Sig Saur 1911, shooting him twice in the chest. Putting back the gun, she pulled out her phone.

"This is Lieutenant Lilah Evans at Freeway Park in downtown. Suspect down. Shots fired by me. Please send patrol and Detective Allen Davies. I'll stay here, with the body."

"Copy. Sending patrol to Freeway Park." The voice cut off.

Lilah dialed another number.

"Hi Doctor Collins, it's Lilah. I need you at Freeway Park to collect a body. It's one of those things I trust you to handle."

"I'll be right there."

After the doctor hung up, Lilah picked up Fenris, moving him to a more visible area. There was blood at the end of the path she was on, and now wasn't the time to explain it. For once, she was glad the urban legend that the "dead don't bleed" was incorrect.

"Lilah?" It was her partner's voice. He'd made it there before the patrol car. She could hear sirens coming their way.

"Davies, over here." As Lilah yelled he turned the corner toward her. She stood over the body, as if protecting it. Davies looked down at it, and then back at Lilah, his eyes angry.

"What the hell Lilah? You were supposed to wait for me, before engaging with a suspect! You could have been hurt! What were you thinking??"

"I'd yell at you for insubordination, but I think you're just worried so I'll let it slide. Fenris here wasn't a suspect at the time. I'd met him while looking for Stephens' killer at *Bebe's* and he called tonight, said he'd found something out. He wanted to meet here, away from work.

"When I got here, he turned on me. He'd taken Rainbow, I could see it in his eyes, and taunted me, that he was the killer, and attacked me. He landed a few punches, before I cleared my weapon. I had no choice but to shoot him. He was trying to kill me too."

Davies looked at her with suspicion.

"Okay, where are the cuts? Somehow he slashed and cut up his victims, so why not you?"

"I have no idea. Perhaps he was working up to it when I shot him. Though I searched him, and he didn't have a sharp object with him. Perhaps he thought he could beat me to death?" Lilah wasn't sure that Davies was buying any of this.

"Perhaps." He sighed. "You know you're going to get mandatory suspension with pay until this shooting is investigated, right?"

"Of course. I know the drill." Fumbling around for a moment, she pulled her gun and badge.

"I'm giving these to you now, in good faith. I relinquish the crime scene, and body to you. If you have any more questions, or need me to speak with whomever, you'll find me at home, sleeping. After this case, I deserve a short vacation anyway." She gave him a wry grin.

"Very well. I'll see you when you return, Sir." Allen Davies enjoyed working with Lilah, and the "Sir" let her know just how much. She smiled, and started walking to the parking lot, leaving the crime scene behind her. Lilah was hoping to talk to Doctor Dru before she went home.

Luck was still on her side, though with everything the sun was beginning to rise, the pink and orange of sunrise could be seen to the East of her. Doctor Dru pulled in just as Lilah hit the parking lot. As she got out, Lilah stopped to talk with her.

"May I have a moment?"

"Of course." Dru turned, and yelled over her shoulder, "Boys get moving, that body isn't going to put itself on the gurney. Just make sure Detective Davies and crew are done with the crime scene before you touch the body."

"This isn't our first day, Doc." Donovan called back jovially. With him was a new assistant. He stayed quiet, and followed Donovan without even a glance her direction. As they walked about, Dru looked at Lilah.

"What?"

"Aren't you going through assistants really quickly?"

Doctor Dru raised an eyebrow, "Is that what you wanted to talk to me about?"

"Of course not," Lilah chuckled a little, letting go of some of the stress of the evening. "You're going to find a body with two bullet holes. Those are mine. On autopsy, you're also going to find a broken neck. I'm asking that you find a plausible reason for it, or make it go away entirely. I can't explain it on my report, not without giving myself away."

"It's one of those. Don't worry, as always, your secret is safe with me." Inwardly, Dru sighed.

"There's one other thing. He was also a werewolf. If something appears in the blood to lead that way, can you hide it as well? Feel free to report that he was on Rainbow."

"I hid it before, with Keith Richmond. Someday, I think I'd like to hear this story."

"Someday, if I can, I'll tell you." Lilah smiled and Dru knew that was the closest to a promise she was going to get.

"Go home Lilah. They'll be calling you tomorrow to do paperwork. Get some sleep."

"That's the plan."

Lilah walked away slowly until she was sure she was out of sight, and then used vampire speed to get home before the light became too cumbersome.

Chapter Twenty-Six

Once home, Lilah felt energized, not tired. She was also worried. She rushed to the full length mirror by her bed to determine how much of her soul she sold to the night to defeat Fenris and save Ulric.

As usual, the first thing she noticed was her eyes, as devoid as ever. The rest of her face was the same one she stared at every morning. Lilah looked herself up and down, finding one difference. Three of her fingers on her right hand, swirled with dark mist in the mirror. Not her chest, not her face, but her fingers. The fingers she'd used to heal Ulric. Lilah had always assumed, should she lose more of her soul, it'd started at the head and work down.

The fingers didn't feel any different. She could move, feel, and use them normally. They weren't quite as dark as her eyes, but they were definitely different. What had happened out there to cause such strange damage? She knew she'd used the night, or some magic contained within to save Ulric. Lilah thought the risk to her soul was worth it. But she was pretty sure her life changed. Even now, safe in her apartment, she could feel what was left of the night. Nowhere would be safe from the pull of magic, of night, and of blood. She planned to keep fighting it, all the same.

It was time for Lilah to find something silly to watch on the television. She'd earned it tonight. As she sat, one thing still bothered her. When she'd gone after Fenris, told him he deserved to die for all the murders, for the pain and destruction caused by his distribution of Rainbow, he started to say something.

"I didn't..." Fenris had seemed startled at the implication that he was responsible for Rainbow in Seattle. Perhaps he wasn't the dealer. Maybe he was just a psychotic murder due to his intake of the drug. That thought unsettled her a little. No one she'd seen take Rainbow got out unscathed, and she feared running into it again.

"Oh well," she said out loud, "as Scarlett O'Hara would say: tomorrow is another day."

More Books
by Gwendolyn Jensen-Woodard

Short Stories

Nightlife

A Seattle Homicide cop works nights – and that is a good thing – she is half-vampire. Detective Lilah Evans gets called to a dead body found just blocks from a nightclub where a girl went missing only hours before. She must find out if there's a connection, and do her damnedest to solve the crime, all while protecting her secret.

Heart of Night

Lady Jannessa Guillory was the daughter of an ambassador, and therefore it was her duty to help her father entertain and manage the household, to marry to her station... and to be ever obedient. Yet, the night called to her in such a way she couldn't deny it. And when a voice found her in the dark, she knew she couldn't stop her own passions.

Translations

French Editions

Au Coeur de la Nuit
Gwendolyn Jensen-Woodard

Lady Jannessa Guillory était la fille d'un Ambassadeur, et par conséquent il était de son devoir envers son père de recevoir et gérer le foyer, pour se marier dans sa position... et être très obéissante. Toutefois, la nuit l'appelait de telle manière qu'elle ne pouvait la nier. Et même une voix la trouvait dans les ténèbres, elle savait qu'elle ne pouvait aller contre ses propres passions.

Spanish Editions

El Corazón de la Noche
Gwendolyn Jensen-Woodard

La señorita Jannessa Guillory era la hija de un embajador y se esperaba de ella que cumpliese con su deber: casarse con una persona de su misma clase y ayudar a su padre. Sin embargo, la noche le llamaba de tal manera que no podía rechazarla. Y cuando una voz la encontró en la oscuridad, sabía que no podía frenar sus pasiones.

 Italian Editions

Vita Notturna
Gwendolyn Jensen-Woodard

Una poliziotta della sezione omicidi di Seattle che lavora di notte - e questa è una buona cosa - ed è per metà vampiro. Il detective Lilah Evans, che deve investigare sul caso di un cadavere trovato a pochi isolati dalla discoteca dove, solo poche ore prima, era scomparsa una ragazza. Deve scoprire se c'è una connessione tra i due eventi e fare l'impossibile per risolvere il caso, il tutto proteggendo il suo segreto.

Portuguese Editions

Coração Noturno
Gwendolyn Jensen-Woodard

Lady Jannessa Guillory era filha de um embaixador e, portanto, era seu dever ajudar seu pai a entreter e a administrar a casa, casar-se com sua função... e sempre ser obediente. Contudo, a noite a atraía de tal forma que ela não podia negar. E quando uma voz a encontrou na escuridão, ela sabia que não poderia parar suas próprias paixões.

 Italian Editions

Il Cuore della Notte
Gwendolyn Jensen-Woodard

Lady Jannessa Guillory era la figlia di un ambasciatore, e pertanto era suo compito aiutare suo padre a gestire e mantenere la casa, sposarsi con qualcuno al suo livello... ed essere sempre obbediente. Eppure la notte la chiamava in un modo che non poteva negare. E quando una voce la trovò nell'oscurità, seppe che non poteva frenare la propria passione.

Gwendolyn Jensen-Woodard lives with her two loves, four dogs, two cats, and a very strange housemate, in the Pacific Northwest. She loves acting, but especially loves writing, which she's been doing since she was twelve.

Where to find Gwendolyn Jensen-Woodard online

Website:
https://AuthorGwendolynJensenWoodard.wordpress.com

Twitter: @gjensenwoodard

Facebook: https://www.facebook.com/GJensenWoodardAuthor

Blog:
https://AuthorGwendolynJensenWoodard.wordpress.com

Ebooks and Audiobooks and Paperbacks, Oh My!

WEBSITE
https://www.VanillaHeartPublishing.com

FACEBOOK #TEAMVHP

VHP BOOK TOURS
http://VHPBookTours.com

TWITTER
@VanillaHeart

www.ingramcontent.com/pod-product-compliance
Lightning Source LLC
Chambersburg PA
CBHW050935120626
46552CB00001B/218